WHISPERS OF SHADOWS

THE RISE OF THE PENGUINS SAGA

STEVEN HAMMOND

ROCKHOPPER BOOKS

WHISPERS OF SHADOWS
Copyright © 2014 Steven Hammond
All rights reserved.
ISBN-10: 0692273999

ISBN-13: 978-0692273999 (Rockhopper Books)
2nd Edition

Edited by Michelle Patricia Browne
Cover art by Caner Inciucu
Interior layout by Tanya Adams

Exclusive content at:
http://riseofthepenguins.com/

Dedicated to

Abby and Kevin, my awesome possoms

ACKNOWLEDGMENTS

I would like to thank all of the usual suspects. Joy for her constant support and encouragement. Kevin and Taylor for spotting my typing deficiencies. Dan and Peggy at the Clovis Book Barn for their unending support of literacy and local authors. Buster dog for keeping me sane. Michelle, Tanya and Caner for all of the effort they put into these books. And thank you to everybody who enjoys my little stories—I appreciate your support more than you know.

THE RISE OF THE PENGUINS SAGA

RISE OF THE PENGUINS

THE WARLORD, THE WARRIOR, THE WAR

CROSSCURRENTS

WHISPERS OF SHADOWS

THE ROYAL CREED

ORDER OF KINGS

THE GREAT AUK WAR (coming soon)

DRAMATIS PENGUINIS

(Eudyptes moseleyi a.k.a. Northern Rockhoppers)

Commander Nok—Commander of the Defense Ministry

Keerka—Council of Order, Advisor

Leeg—Fledgling son of Nok and Keerka

Kicki—Fledgling female

Tearsk—Adolescent male, crèche minder

Sergeant Trarck—Council Sergeant

Packt—Colony matriarch, Council Member

Cosk—Council Member

Melk—Council Member

Cleyed—Council Member

Lydeck—Council Member

Trasik-lon—Council member

Kerl—Council Member

Kank—Council Member

Colonel Kairg—Commanding Officer

Lieutenant Ki-ok—Officer of the Ministry

Sergeant Kuk-kek

Tretak

ROCKHOPPER COLONY 23

NORTH SHORE

KELP GOOSE MARSH

GENTOO RISE

PETREL LANDING

LAST STAND

SHADOW BREACH

WARRENS

BLACK SAND BEACH

TUSSET GRASS SLOPE

CARACARA WRECK

N
W E
S

Each new day calls the shadows back from the dead.
—Mahak-chig-rantoo, The Guardian of Realms

WHISPERS OF SHADOWS

CHAPTER 1

Rockhopper Colony 23: three months after the death of the Overlord. A bullet ricocheted off of the rock in front of Commander Nok's beak as he dashed between outcrops on the cliff.

"Will you get back in here," Keerka warned Nok. "You're no good to us if you're dead."

"Hah! I doubt that. Some of the greatest leaders are martyrs who led the masses to greater truths from the Great Sea."

"You've hung around those Gentoo philosophizers for far too long." A series of bullets peppered the rocks. Keerka ducked for cover in the crag they were hiding in.

Nok jumped out, waved his flippers and dove back. More gunshots rang out. "They're relentless today," Nok said.

Keerka shook her head at his ill-advised bravado. "They've been relentless for over a month now. I'm pretty sure that's all our son knows. He hasn't even had the chance to explore the outside."

Nok nuzzled Keerka, wishing these men would just go away so they could all live in peace—so Leeg, their son, could know the peace that Nok never had. But he knew the odds of that happening were about the same as a Gentoo keeping its beak shut for more than two breaths. "Leeg will be fine. This will be over soon and he and his friends will be able to bounce all over outside instead of causing trouble in here. But for right now we have to stick to the plan. The humans are becoming more brazen in their attacks. In fact, the time to strike back might be here. But without the support of the AIC, we have to be smart about our attack. We had twice as many Rockhoppers and the support of the Gentoo last time."

Nok prepared to jump out again, but a bullet grazing his head-plume made him think twice. He looked at Keerka, who let out a relieved sigh. He looked at his mate and saw something more than concern about him getting shot in her eyes. "What has your thoughts?"

Keerka hesitated. "Lydeck is rabblerousing about your leadership again. He's saying you've waited too long to act and that you've lost your fight."

"Bah, when hasn't he rabble-roused?" Nok shook his head then gave his mate an earnest look. "Is that what you think…that I've lost my fight?"

"No. Absolutely not. You're the Commander of the Defense Ministry. You hold authority over the Council of Order and the Tribunal. This new position of Commander is a bigger burden than even General Treeg could have imagined. Your decisions impact the entire colony. We both know what's at stake if this escalates. Lydeck has only seen what happened here before the war, which was horrible. But he has no idea of what the humans are truly capable of—the power of their weapons. He wasn't with us."

"The Rockhoppers have always bickered between each other, but never to this degree. I don't know what has Lydeck's tail-feathers in a bunch. He's becoming ambitious—too ambitious if you ask me. If I didn't know better, I'd swear he had been trained by the Royals."

"I think he might want your job."

Nok shook his head. "The Council would sooner elect a Kelp Goose."

"They elected you."

Nok ignored the comment and poked his head out from behind the rock and pulled back just before several bullets pinged off the stone. "Daylight is waning. Do you think we've distracted them enough?"

"I think so. They should be out to sea by now. Hopefully they'll be able to fill their stomachs and feed their young," Keerka said.

Nok couldn't help but to stick his head out once more and give the men a grating call. He was rewarded by an intense barrage of gunfire.

"Was that really necessary?" Keerka said, eyeing him sternly.

Nok gave her a mischievous look. "No, but it sure is funny. They get so mad."

Nok and Keerka turned and walked down a dark corridor inside the Defense Ministry. The stolen lanterns which had once illuminated the interior of the warrens were nearly all gone, with reserves used for upper command and vital areas. General Treeg had always found a way to raid human camps or pillage shipwrecks, but the men rarely came aground any more. The war had left the nearby Falkland Islands nearly desolate and the Argentinians had become eager to restart the conflict against the British for control over the disputed islands. The British forces became less concerned about pursuing penguins and more interested in securing its territory. In spite being told otherwise, the locals knew through rumor and tales that the island known as *La Isla de los Pingüinos de la Muerte* harbored penguins that responded to attacks with equal violence. Unfettered by law, men no longer came for poaching—they came for the sport of killing.

"You go to the ministry, I'll go check on Leeg," Keerka said.

"You are an important part of the Council as well. You may not be a full member but you're as trusted of an advisor as that old sea-hag Packt."

"I'm done with the Council. I can advise you from the nest. Go…have fun."

Nok watched her leave while she waved his comments away. He knew what she was doing for him and the faith she had in him, not only as the Rockhopper Commander, but as a mate and a father to their son. He watched her walk toward the crèche with silent appreciation and wondered how long he would've survived without her.

"Sergeant Trarck, call for the Council," Nok said as he entered the ministry chamber.

"Is it time, Commander?" Sergeant Trarck asked eagerly.

"It may be. If not now then very soon," Nok said. Trarck's enthusiasm brought on a touch of melancholy. He was only a couple of seasons younger than Nok and even though Trarck had seen some of the atrocities of the humans, he hadn't experienced the full scale warfare that Nok had. He wished he could get a bit of that innocence back.

When Trarck scuffled away, Nok heard the sound of his mate's feet return all too soon. "Where is Leeg?" he asked.

"Apparently off on another adventure. He is your son," Keerka said.

"That is true," Nok sighed. "But unlike his mother, I never longed for adventure."

CHAPTER 2

"Keep up, Kicki," the stout, fluffy, gray, Rockhopper penguin chick said.

"I'm trying. You're all a few days older than me. I don't have your bounce yet," said Kicki. She had often heard Nok say Leeg and her were as inseparable as water and wet, whatever that meant. Leeg was her best friend and that's all that mattered. "Where are we going, anyways?"

Leeg slid back down the rock he had just ascended. In a dramatic whisper, he replied, "We're going to the cave of the Mahak-chig-rantoo. He is the guardian between realms; between our world and the Ancients."

Kicki looked at Leeg sideways. "And he happens to live here on this island? In a cave within a cave of the Defense Ministry? I don't believe that for a second," she said in a huff as she hopped down to the next stone.

"He doesn't live here, for he is neither living nor dead. A realm guardian has no life and only exists to protect the gateway between realms," Leeg said, bouncing around Kicki.

"And what is he or *she* protecting it from? If no one is supposed to know about the gateway he has to get awfully bored."

"He's not protecting it from those who go in. He's keeping those who want out from returning to the realm of the living." Leeg whooped, bouncing around Kicki.

"If nobody is supposed to know about it, then how did *you* find out about it?" Kicki asked.

Leeg stopped bouncing and looked around to make sure the others were out of ear shot. "The crèche minder told me."

"Which one? Tearsk?" Kicki demanded.

Leeg looked at Kicki wide-eyed, with a hint of doubt. "Yeah. Why?"

"Honestly, Leeg. I think the only reason Tearsk took the position of crèche minder was to torment little fledgling boys like you. I can't believe we're exploring because of a story he told."

"Well there wouldn't be any reason for exploring if we knew for sure, would there?"

Kicki began to walk down the path but stopped. "No, there wouldn't." Something nagged at the back of her mind. She dismissed it.

"Do you still want to go see?"

"Of course I do," she answered a little too loudly. She cringed as her voice echoed off of the stone walls of the cavern.

Leeg snorted. "All right then, let's go. But beware; I heard a story that one of the Overlord's Shadow Warriors was lost in these very chambers. He, too, is looking for the cave of the Mahak-chig-rantoo. He is trying to return his dead master, the Overlord, back to the realm of the living." Leeg began hopping and whooping around Kicki again while she walked.

"Well if *he* hasn't found it yet, then I'm pretty sure we won't have any better luck."

"Bah. My dad says that a Rockhopper can outsmart a Royal Emperor any old day. If it's here, we'll find it."

"If what's here—the cave or the Shadow Warrior?" Kicki asked. She began to feel a little more than nervous about the adventure now that a Royal Emperor had been mentioned. A silent tickle in the back of her mind nagged at her.

"Either one," Leeg said. "I'm not afraid. My dad help defeat Liutites. And you shouldn't be either. Your mother helped defeat Diutes. It's in our blood to kill Royals."

"I'm not afraid," she whispered. Feeling vulnerable away from the crèche, she urged Leeg to catch up to the others. She glanced back at the way they had come.

CHAPTER 3

The interior of the Defense Ministry's Council of Order chamber flickered and danced. Light from a dozen lanterns bounced off of slate gray stone walls, outcroppings and ledges. Flashlights; some with the backing of tin-plates to act as reflectors, cast the dull light of dying batteries. The lights made odd shadows dance around the natural nearly circular room. Centuries-old Rockhopper claw marks indicated paths in the stone on either side of the chamber. Raised voices and calls echoed throughout as the perpetually squabbling Rockhoppers argued over nesting sites, hunting spots or even the possibility of rain.

During General Treeg's reign, most of the squabbling had subsided. But since the venerated old Rockhopper's death on Isla Sola, the clan had fallen into disarray. Some of the members of the Defense Ministry thought Nok was unfit as their leader, while some argued that as Treeg's only surviving kin, even though he had been adopted, it was Nok's rightful position. After an almost unanimous vote of nine to one, Nok had been appointed to the newly created position of Commander and given the eleventh seat on the council. Being that Nok's supporters held a majority on the council, most of Nok's few initiatives had passed. But under the constant assault of the humans, support had begun to wane for the war hero. Action had been called for and his most adamant detractor, Lydeck, began to gain support.

Commander Nok paced on his platform, near the head of the chamber, perfectly placed between the higher platforms of the senior members of the Council and the lower platforms holding the junior members. Sergeant Trarck stood watching his friend and commander with admiration and the expectancy of great things to come. Nok seemed oblivious to all things, including the other members of the Defense Ministry's Council of Order as they entered none-too-quietly.

"Sir, relax," Trarck said after having enough of Nok's nervous fidgeting. "You still have the support of the majority. Cosk, Melk, Cleyed and even that old frump Packt is in your nest. It will be fine."

Nok stopped his pacing and sighed. "Well Cleyed credits me for saving Melk. And honestly, the thought of Packt in my nest is the stuff of nightmares. But seriously, whether I have the support of the Council or not doesn't really matter at this point. The time has come and it will cost Rockhopper lives. I'm not too keen on sending our families to die." He kept his eyes averted.

"Trust yourself, Commander. Hundreds of Rockhoppers do and thousands of other penguins did during your time in the AIC."

"I never wanted this—the death of so many, war against the humans, or even leadership. Yes, there was a time when vengeance consumed my thoughts, but after the war and the rebellion against the Royals, I just don't have that fire any longer." He stopped himself from saying more from fear that it would diminish Trarck's view of him.

"And that's what makes you a great leader. You genuinely care for the wellbeing of us all. That's why we look to you. It's not just about being the great warrior you were and still are."

Nok eyed his friend, appreciating his kindness. "All I want now is peace. I want us to be safe, to be able to raise our young free of these attacks; free from war, death and destruction. I just want Leeg and all of our sons and daughters to live without fear. We have enough worries without walking straight into death's eager beak like a cloud of krill." He thought of Treeg, Leepoh, Mevoule and so many others who had lost their lives during the ill-advised campaign against the humans and uprising against the Royals. He thought of Lavour and wondered where he might be and if he had found that peace along with Meuseaux. Maybe Lavour had the right idea; maybe the only path to peace was to swim away, far away, where war couldn't follow. He envied that freedom, but the thought of his family brought him back to reality. He knew he wouldn't trade that for all of the freedom in the world.

"And we will have that. Maybe not today, maybe not in our lifetimes, but one day it will come," said Trarck.

"I truly hope so," Nok said. "Let's call this assembly to order."

At Sergeant Trarck's call, the raucous caws of the birds ceased. All of the Rockhoppers took their respective places and stood with beaks held high.

"In keeping with the tradition of those who have come and gone before us, we will begin with an invocation," Commander Nok said. "Cosk will lead us in this tribute."

A stout Rockhopper whose long yellow head plumage draped down along the sides of his face walked to the center of the chamber and spread his flippers out wide. "Rockhoppers of the Defense Ministry and Council of Order, let us hold our assembly in the spirit of peace and goodwill toward one another. Never forgetting that the Great Spirit of the Ancients swims at our sides through all of our worldly endeavors and guides our hearts through the multitude of tribulations placed upon our mortal lives. And forever keep in mind that, though we may be separate in body, we are unified in heart. Hold this truth within you, always." Cosk concluded the benediction by lowering his head and wings. The Council replied in unison with, *May the Spirits of the Ancients be at our sides.*

"Thank you, Cosk. Eloquent as always," Nok said while Cosk returned to his place. Nok looked around the assembly, taking the time study the faces of every member. His eyes came to rest on Lydeck, who returned his gaze through narrowed eyes. When it appeared as if Lydeck was about to open his beak, the commander began, "As has happened to many of us, when I was just a fledgling, my mother and father were taken by the humans. From that moment on, the pain of loss was forever etched into my being. If not for General Treeg, I too might have joined them in The Great Sea. We are a collection of orphans, of widows and widowers, of adoptees of kind and caring Rockhoppers. We are a group of proud and determined penguins, who must, for our survival, always remain united. When General Treeg first formed the Defense Ministry, it was under the auspicious idea that we would take control of our destiny. Each and every Rockhopper had a responsibility to one another. We should act as a united colony. The old ways of bickering over trivial matters were to be put aside for the good of the community. Other clans followed our example. The Penguin Defense Alliance came into being, and soon all of the clans became one.

"Unfortunately, in spite all of his good intentions, Treeg didn't know the full power of the humans, nor did he know that the Overlord and the Royal Emperors had their own designs. He learned this just before his life was taken. Many of us experienced the brutality of the war and learned that war is, at best, a feeble effort to control the world we live in. During my travels I have learned a great deal about the humans. Their numbers are incomprehensible. They own this world, and the reality of that knowledge suggests that we merely exist in another creature's world. We can never hope to truly defeat them. Humans will always be humans, and they will always kill." Nok paused to gauge the reaction of the council. Several members shuffled nervously and others, like Lydeck, fixed Nok with an unreadable stare.

"But that does not mean that we should stand idly by while they kill us for sport," Nok continued. "While I was at PIC, I learned of the way the Royals dealt with their ancient enemy, the Phocids or as we know them, the Leopard Seals. While I don't agree with their methods, there was some value. The seals were lured into complacency. When the moment was right, they dealt a decisive blow and eradicated a large portion of the beasts. My fellow Rockhoppers, the humans have become complacent. They do not fear us and they have faith in their weapons. These are not the same type of humans we faced on the islands to the north, the Falklands. They do not have the flying machines which killed so many of us. But, as we can all attest to, they are very capable of dealing death. At this moment, there are three human vessels waiting off shore. They all carry the raiders who have tormented our colony these past two moons. Keeping in mind that they have become complacent, I believe that the time to strike is tomorrow when they come ashore. But I will not make this decision for everyone. I am not a dictator like the former Overlord. The decision to strike must be put to a vote before the Council."

The council members began to chatter. Rockhoppers warbled and brayed at one another, and pinfeathers flew. The Commander knew that he was breaking precedent to what Treeg had established as leader of the Council of Order. Treeg had made the decision to attack without a vote. But that was a different time, and unlike General Treeg, Nok didn't want to shoulder the burden alone.

Nok returned to his place and looked at Sergeant Trarck, who went to the center of the chamber.

"Order. Order!" Trarck shouted. After the noisy crowd calmed, Trarck continued, "A motion has been put before the Council. Discussion."

"Question," Lydeck said, not bothering to go to center. "Why now? Why haven't we struck before now? Is it that you fear losing your position of Commander? That you fear that the Rockhoppers are beginning to doubt your leadership? Do you feel the shift in momentum, Commander Nok?"

Another uproar resumed among the members.

Once quiet resumed Nok spoke. "Lydeck, my friend, you know that I have no such fear. My fear only pertains to the certain loss of life which is inevitable during such a fight. Regardless of how you may feel about me personally, you know that I have only what is best for us in mind. I believe I have explained that. Or were your thoughts elsewhere?"

"If you fear such a loss of life, then why not a surprise attack on their vessels like before? That would make the most sense," asked Kerl. Although she could be easily swayed, she still supported Nok. She followed her question by looking across the chamber at Trasik-lon, a strong, virile male and the youngest member of the council.

Nok and Trarck took notice of the exchange. "I know whose eggs she'll be laying next season," Nok said quietly to the sergeant.

"Well Commander Nok? Why haven't we slipped aboard the human ships and run them aground as before? An answer, Commander Nok; I am late for my nap."

"I understand, Packt. Your naps are your most productive hours these days," Nok jibed at her. Packt snorted. The ribbings were all in good spirits, but to those who weren't in on the joke, it appeared differently. "The answer is simple. With the Gentoo gone and with the heavy losses our colony took during the war, we simply do not have the numbers to launch a successful strike. And keep in mind that we were fortuitous during that attack. The previous human ship was more easily accessed, and even then we had to use the swells from the storm to clear the sides."

The room erupted into a chorus of squawking once again until Lydeck called the crowd to order. A hush fell, and all eyes focused on the Rockhopper as he walked to the center of the chamber. "Commander Nok, we have heard your speech and received *some* answers, but what we haven't heard is any real strategy on eliminating these particular humans from our island. I know of your fear of battle now, and I believe I understand some of it. But *I* fear that you have become hesitant, if not outright fearful, and I believe that your trepidation will lead us to our demise."

Nok bristled at being accused of trepidation, but he knew Lydeck was trying to rile him. What he couldn't figure out was why. Sure, Lydeck had been the chief penguin in mustering support against Nok's leadership. "Lydeck… It is just Lydeck still? Unless, of course, you have achieved a military rank of which I am unaware."

Lydeck glared at Nok. "No. You are correctly aware that I have not."

"Very well. I was once told by a wise penguin that only a fool does not fear his enemy. It is the fear that produces the ability to fight. Not the anger as one would expect. Vengeance can give you sufficient motivation, but it is the fear which sustains your energy for combat—the fear of death, the fear of your comrade's death and the fear of your enemy's victory. Until recently, and then only for a short time, the humans had a fear of us. And that fear gave them a sharp edge. They were alert for attacks and no attacks have come. Now they have no fear, while we still do. We now have an edge over them."

Lydeck inwardly smirked. "Are you telling us that you are afraid, Commander? Is that the reason for your inaction against these raiders?" he said, turning to the crowd.

Nok looked at the faces gathered for the forum. "Of course I fear them, Lydeck. I'm no fool."

"Nor am I," Lydeck replied sharply. "But only a fool stands by and lets those who look to him for leadership die, if for no other reason than to lure the enemy into complacency!"

"If we attacked before now, many more would die. As it stands today, many more will die during the fighting. The burden of the death of our kind is not something I carry lightly. Now enough of this pointless rabble-rousing; a motion has been brought before the Council. Is there any further discussion?"

The old matriarch, Packt, rose from her haunches to speak once again. "I propose that we table the motion until a reconnoiter is performed so that we have an accurate assessment of our enemy's strength."

The council, led by Lydeck, erupted into loud cackles screaming of collusion between Nok and Packt to avoid the vote.

"Order," Trarck called. "We will have order!"

Nok thanked his sergeant and stepped forward. A Rockhopper messenger darted into the room and quietly spoke to the Commander.

Nok let out a breath in irritation. "We will take a brief recess, after which we will *civilly* discuss Packt's motion." Without further word, Nok left the Council chamber.

CHAPTER 4

"Where has he gone to this time?" Nok asked, annoyed, as he met Keerka in the corridor to the chamber.

"To the far reaches below the warrens," Keerka said, hiding her anxiety. "Apparently the Crèche-minder has been telling stories again."

"Tearsk?" Now Nok was angry. "We need to find a new minder. Who placed him in that position anyways?"

Keerka looked at Nok accusingly.

Nok averted his eyes. "I felt I owed it to his father. I guess I'll be more conscious of who I give political favors to next time."

"How is the meeting going?"

"A motion is on the floor to decide whether or not we go on the offensive. Lydeck is, of course, trying to rile up the others. I have a feeling that he may be making a play for my seat. Packt is being surprisingly vocal today. But I've called a recess; now we have to find Leeg—it's dangerous down there."

"Don't worry about that. I already have a team assembled," Keerka said.

Nok hesitated. "All right then. You be careful." He looked at his mate and a thought occurred to him. "And take Tearsk along with you. It'll do him good to learn what his stories do to the young ones."

As Nok watched Keerka leave, Packt's voice interrupted his thoughts.

He let out a heavy breath and turned to face her without saying a word.

"You're tired and yet you're not old, Nok," Packt said as she lead the commander to a side passage.

"Astute observation as always, Packt," Nok said.

"Nok, Nok, Nok, Nok...Nok," Packt said, slowly walking along the corridor. "I sound like I'm rapping on a piece of driftwood, don't I?"

Commander Nok said nothing at first, but could not keep it that way. "Is there a point to your calling me aside? There's a motion we really should vote on," he said with lighter tone.

Packt ignored Nok's comment. "I need to discuss something with you privately."

Nok looked around, seeing they were alone, and almost made another sarcastic comment but thought better of it. "What is it?"

"We all know of the prophecy—the one who will lead us to peace. And you and I both know it wasn't the Overlord," Packt said.

"True. It was Lavour," said Nok.

Packt shifted her corpulent frame from side to side. "Perhaps...perhaps not."

Nok wasn't quite sure how to respond. It was under Lavour's leadership that they had defeated the Royals; or at least the Overlord and Liutites. He thought about it more and realized if the humans had not bombed them to the underworld, then they would have likely never had the opportunity to take down Liutites. And it wasn't just Lavour who had defeated him. It was himself, Lavour, Meuseaux and Leepoh. The thought of Leepoh gave Nok a fresh pang in his heart. Time still hadn't softened the loss of his friends. The thought of Leepoh's death seemed to hurt the worst. He shook off the thoughts of his friends—that was the past, and he had plenty to deal with in the present. "Are you saying the prophecy could refer to a Rockhopper? Because if you're implying it's me, then you're swimming in low tide. I am *not* the one the fortune-teller was talking about."

"The Oracle is not a fortune-teller. What I'm saying is that maybe each clan has to find their own way, their own leader or the one who will deliver them." Packt paused, lowered her head, and seemed to fall asleep. Nok cocked his head in confusion. She abruptly opened her eyes and lifted her head, startling Nok. "When Cryftin foretold the—"

"Who is Cryftin?" Nok interrupted.

"Cryftin is the voice of the Oracle, Lapasia. He told the story to several clan Elders just before the Great Wave took them both away. When Cryftin departed, Antaean seized the opportunity and claimed to be the one he spoke of."

Nok shook his head. "It really doesn't matter, because the one who foretold all of this is dead. We can never know for certain."

"I never said that Cryftin or the Oracle were dead, only that the wave took them."

"So they're alive?" Nok asked. If this Cryftin and Lapasia were still alive, then maybe the truth could be found. It was tempting to seek them out. If the Oracle truly was what she was made out to be, then it all could be settled once and for all. Nok pushed the thought away. He had to focus on the here and now. Besides, finding them would be like searching for a raindrop in the sea.

"I didn't say that either. You're right; the truth is… it doesn't matter. They could still be out there on some lonely atoll waiting for someone to find them so they can deliver the truth. But Cryftin in particular was old before I was old, and chances are he has long since gone to the Great Sea. What I'm saying to you is that you could aspire to the loftiness that is needed by our kind. Tell me; how do you truly feel about this proposed attack tomorrow?"

Nok hesitated. Was this all some ploy set up by the opposition? It could be, but something in his gut told him to take a leap of faith. "I have a feeling it could turn out to be a disaster," he finally said.

"As do I. There is a great chance of failure." Packt studied Nok for moment as if gauging what to say next. "If the Council approves your motion, the attack will happen, and it will no longer be within your control."

"But if I don't act now, the Council will likely replace me with Lydeck," Nok said.

"Great leaders not only have to have the courage to make the decisions that will make them popular, they also have to have the courage to make the decisions that will make them despised by those they are sworn to protect."

"But—"

"There are no more buts. You must trust your instincts, whether it is about yourself or another." Packt paused and again seemed to nod off while Nok waited. "Fortune looms, Nok. Fortuitous events may transpire very soon. Be prepared. Another Oracle is burgeoning. She must be protected."

Packt said no more, leaving Nok alone to digest all that she had told him. *Fortune looms?* "Whatever that means," Nok said. The scream of fighter jets passing over the island, as they often had since the outbreak of hostilities between Great Britain and Argentina, snapped Nok back to reality. It was a reality he didn't want to face just yet, but he had no choice.

"Call the Council from recess, Sergeant Trarck," Nok said, entering a slightly less raucous Council chamber.

Trarck surveyed the room. "Council member Lydeck has not returned just yet."

The muffled scream of jet engines silenced the crowd. Nok let out an irritated breath. "We're wasting daylight, Sergeant. Call the Council to order. We'll consider Lydeck's vote as abstained."

"He won't like that."

"Then he should be here. Let's get this done."

In a rare show of solidarity, the Council voted unanimously in favor of the motion. As soon as the chamber emptied, Nok took Trarck aside and explained the situation. Together, they hurried toward the crèche with the hope catching Keerka before she went in search of the fledglings.

CHAPTER 5

"I can hardly see," Kicki said, the other fledglings hushing her as she spoke. "I don't know why we have to be quiet. It's not like there is anything down here."

"The Shadow Warrior is here," Leeg chimed in. "He's as big as the Overlord and his feathers are all black. You won't be able to see him. But if you're not quiet, he'll know you're here."

"Isn't that the point? And if he's been here all of this time, what does he eat? A penguin needs to eat."

"You're taking all of the fun out of this," said Leeg.

"Speaking of eating, I'm getting hungry—we were supposed to be back already."

Leeg stopped walking and looked at Kicki, barely making out her features in the dim light. "Do you wanna rest? I'm tired too."

"Well, if you're tired too…"

If the lighting were better, Kicki would have seen the smile in Leeg's eyes. Leeg called to the others telling them that they would wait for them where they were. He received a disinterested *whatever* in return. The two sat in silence for all of two minutes when Leeg had to talk. "If you close your eyes real tight then open them, you can see a little better."

Kicki tried it. "Hey! It works," she said, surprised. "Do you just want to go back?"

"I guess so. I'm getting hungry too."

The pair abandoned their waiting spot and began the slow trek back. After a few minutes, Leeg stopped. "I don't recognize this place," he said.

"Were we supposed take a left or a right at that round rock?"

"We went left on the way down, so we were supposed to go left on the way back…right?"

Kicki shook her head. "Let's go back the way we came."

After several minutes of walking and not seeing the round rock, they had to admit that they might be lost. The friends waited in the darkness, frightened and embarrassed.

"Wait," Leeg said. "I smell water."

"Water?" Kicki asked.

"Yeah. This way." Leeg walked ahead along an upward sloping path. He spotted a slightly brighter opening. "If there's water, then it has to lead out."

"Or it leads in," countered Kicki.

The pair crept slowly forward. As they approached the opening, they picked up the unmistakable scent of sea water.

"Do you think this is the cave of Mahak-chig-rantoo?" Kicki asked, mocking the story. She stopped, her head swaying. "Leeg, wait. Don't go in there. It's dangerous."

Leeg didn't reply; he waved his flipper at her to hush. Something had caught his eye just beyond the opening. Below him, near the back of the nearly thirty meter wide cave, two vague forms could be seen in mist—one unmistakably a Rockhopper and the other much larger. They appeared to be in conversation. A pool of water glimmered ever so slightly in the center and to the left lay a heap of freshly broken stones, as if the wall had recently crumbled. Wind moaned through the breach, drowning out the conversation.

Kicki came to Leeg's side and spotted what had him so transfixed. "Is that the Guardian?" She hadn't believed the fairy tales, but she did not expect to actually see anybody down there.

"Quiet," Leeg said in a whisper. He slipped through the opening.

"What are you doing?" Kicki said, matching his whisper. Not wanting to be left alone, she followed him inside. "This isn't fun anymore. Let's get out of here. Something bad is going to happen."

"It's the Shadow Warrior," Leeg said, even quieter than before. "My father needs to know about it."

"He won't know about it if we're dead. Let's go," Kicki demanded.

Leeg couldn't argue with her reasoning. "All right. But I want to see who it's talking to." He scurried into a crag a little further in, Kicki close on his tail. As she moved to join him, she kicked a small stone and watched helplessly as it bounced down the angled rocks. She pressed her body against the rocks, her light gray plumage blending in with her surroundings, and stared at Leeg fearfully. When she finally glanced back to the shadowy figures, they were gone. Her heart raced in panic. Not knowing what else to do, she abandoned her post and joined Leeg in the crag.

Leeg and Kicki laid on their bellies and tried to remain motionless. From his vantage point, Leeg could see the pool, but he could hear only the fitful gasps of the wind. He narrowed his eyes to filter out the surrounding shapes and caught a motion. The large, dark figure rose from the pool and began a slow walk up the sloping rocks toward where they had been.

The figure came to a stop just beyond the crag. Leeg knew at once that it had to be the Shadow Warrior. The two young Rockhoppers held their breath, fearing that even a breath would betray their position. The sound of webbed feet landing on the rock above them almost betrayed them.

"It was just a falling rock," the voice from above said.

The Royal Emperor Shadow Warrior snapped his head toward the speaker. "Rocks do not fall on their own accord," he said, lifting his beak up as if sniffing the air.

Leeg couldn't recognize the voice of the one standing above them. It was a Rockhopper; of that he was certain, but he didn't know who.

After a few moments of silence, the Rockhopper spoke again. "Then how did that hole get there? There's no one here."

The Shadow Warrior didn't respond. It stood motionless, like a predator about to strike.

"This is getting too dangerous. I should go," the Rockhopper said.

"Don't back out on us now, Rockhopper. If you want the humans gone, we are the only way," the Royal Emperor threatened. "When she arrives, she will bring an army large enough to defeat any resistance."

"And if she doesn't? She could have been killed or decided to make her way to that fabled Northern Paradise."

"She will come," the warrior demanded. "And when she does, and *if* you have control over the Ministry, you will be exalted. As you know, the PDA is still under Royal control. She knows the folly of concentrating our forces in a single stronghold; even General Diutes knew that simple truth."

"Are you sure that the new Overlord will be forgiving of the Rockhoppers? It was our colony who killed Diutes."

"It is already done. You take control of your council—that is your only concern."

"It's already in motion. Once Nok gets his vote and the attack on the humans fails, the council will vote him out and me in. I have guarantees on that," the Rockhopper assured him.

The echo of distant voices stopped all further discussion.

"I have to go," the Rockhopper said, bounding away.

The Shadow Warrior stood where he was, glancing at the surrounding rocks. He clicked menacingly and lowered his head toward the crag. The sound of voices echoed once more. The Shadow Warrior turned his head toward the noise, then slid down the rocks to the pool and disappeared.

After a few minutes Leeg found the courage to talk. "I thought we were done for," he said, letting out a deep breath.

Kicki shook her head. "This isn't fun, Leeg."

"I'm not going to argue with you," Leeg replied.

Kicki craned her head. "Listen…that sounds like your mother. Let's get out of here."

"We have to tell my father," Leeg said, happy to face Keerka's scolding rather than the Shadow Warrior.

Kicki only nodded, too afraid to say anything more.

CHAPTER 6

Keerka led her team of Rockhoppers into the deep and seldom seen reaches of the warrens, Tearsk moaning and complaining all the while.

At hearing the sound of cackling fledglings, Keerka let out a much relieved breath. When she approached the group, she put aside relief and put on her stern adult face. "Where have you been?"

The youths stammered.

"I asked you a question and I expect an answer," Keerka demanded. She scanned the group and didn't spot her son. "Where's Leeg?"

"He said he was going to go back," one the fledglings finally said.

"No, he said they were gonna wait for us," said another.

"Well, which is it?" Keerka asked, concealing her anxiety.

"I think he said they'd wait for us, but I don't remember where," another fledgling answered.

"Was Kicki with him?" Keerka asked, though she already knew the answer.

"Yeah," one of the boys answered, suppressing a laugh. "They're probably rubbing beaks somewhere where no one can find them." The group burst into laughter.

"That is enough!" Keerka roared. The group fell silent. "You are all on restriction until further notice. If you leave the crèche without permission, you *and* your parents will answer to me. Do you understand?"

Wide, fearful eyes glimmered in the dark. It was all the group could do to nod their heads.

"One of you take them back to the crèche," Keerka snapped. Tearsk turned to lead the group back, but Keerka stopped him. "Oh no, not you. You're with me until I find my son and Kicki. Once we do, I will decide on your punishment."

Tearsk swallowed hard. As intimidating as Keerka could be to a fledgling, her almost jovial air toward the idea of him accompanying her into the darkness had a similar effect on the adolescent male. Tearsk lowered his head and walked forward while Keerka eyed him. He raised his head as if to argue but caught Keerka's stern look and thought better of it. With the collection of youngsters safely away, Keerka led her group down the dark path.

CHAPTER 7

Hearing Keerka's distant voice, Lydeck came to a halt. Keerka was smart and not easily fooled. Some had even gone as far as to say that she was the penguin who was best suited for the position of Commander. Lydeck chortled. He, like most others who bothered to pay attention, knew that Nok and Keerka were a team. Lydeck's chortle turned to a frustrated grunt. Keerka would ask too many questions if she were to find him down here by himself. He made his way toward the voices and disappeared into a dark gap. He had no choice but to hide until the group passed.

When the group neared, he strained to hear what was being said. It seemed that none had noticed his disappearance, which made him feel at once both relived but disappointed. He listened as Keerka berated Tearsk for letting Leeg and Kicki wander off.

The Shadow Warrior had heard something in the cave... he cursed himself silently. If the Commander's son overheard him talking to the Shadow, no amount of convincing would make the Council vote him into the position of commander. Once he was certain that the group was a safe distance away, Lydeck slipped out of the darkness and hastily made his was back up to the warrens. He had been gone far too long, and he was sure his presence would be missed by the Council at least. When he reached the entrance, he heard the scuttling of more Rockhopper claws coming his way. Nok . . . it had to be Nok.

His suspicions were confirmed when he heard Nok's voice telling Sergeant Trarck to gather a search party. With nowhere to hide, Lydeck turned his back and began slowly walking back down into the lower reaches. He heard Nok call his name and he turned back to face him. "Yes, Commander Nok?" he asked, his mind racing to find the right lie.

"What are you doing down here? The Council was expecting you back from recess," Nok said, eyeing the other suspiciously.

Lydeck stared at Nok, buying a few more seconds. "I overheard that some of the fledglings were lost. I thought I might be of assistance."

Nok looked him over. "Why would you care? You have no fledglings. This is for the security detail."

"The safety of all Rockhoppers is my concern, Commander. Be that as it may, the sooner we find the Commander's son, the sooner we can take the vote. Such a distraction serves to put the colony's safety into further jeopardy." Nok grunted in frustration and Lydeck did his best to mask his satisfaction.

"If you had returned from recess as you should have, you would have known that the vote was tabled until we have the chance to reconnoiter."

"My apologies, Commander Nok. At risk of personal embarrassment, the feeding runs being so sporadic recently have been hard on my digestion. Nighttime feedings do throw one off track. I was indisposed." Lydeck could almost feel the fire burning in Nok's eyes as he struggled to keep himself under control. His jabs at Nok's leadership had their desired effect, but seeing Nok's eyes slowly turn to rage, he thought he may have pushed it too far. Too his surprise, Nok took a deep breath and the intensity dissipated.

Nok waited to speak as another RAF jet screamed over the island. "It is unfortunate and more than a little inconvenient, but it is in our best interest for the time being. You never know; with the humans at war with each other, they might accidentally blast the raiders straight to the underworld," Nok said as several more fighters passed over.

"Waiting around for an accident is not a prudent policy."

"We are all here by happy accidents, Lydeck," Nok continued in an overly cheerful tone, not allowing himself to be baited. "But if you will excuse me, I have pressing business. Are you still coming along?"

Lydeck stared at Nok. If Nok's son *had* spotted him, it would be prudent for him to keep his distance for the time being. "No. You seem to have the situation under control. I'll take my leave now. Good hunting, Commander." Lydeck turned away without waiting for a reply.

^^^

Nok watched Lydeck walk away and failed to notice Sergeant Trarck's imposing frame enter the corridor. "The search team will be here shortly," Trarck said.

Nok suppressed a jerk. "Good job, Sergeant. You can come with me."

After several minutes of walking in silence, Nok spoke. "Do we have anybody we can trust? Someone who could get in with certain individuals and report back?"

The question caught Trarck by surprise because of the implications. The sergeant waited a few moments before answering. "You wish to spy on Lydeck?"

"Yes," Nok said rather bluntly. "He's up to something and I have a feeling it's more than just trying to have me ousted. I want to find out what it is."

Trarck scanned the cavern and leaned in close. "What makes you say that?"

Nok watched Trarck. The sergeant was as powerfully built as any penguin he had seen and not only Rockhoppers; and he was more intelligent than most. Nok was glad he could be counted as a friend. "Just a hunch, Sergeant. When I ran into him he seemed startled—overly nervous and a little out of breath. He said he was going to help with the search, but when I asked him to come with me, he declined." Something was itching in the back of his mind, but it was an itch he couldn't scratch.

"Well, helping a political adversary might not help him with his campaign," Trarck said, then lowered his voice. "But still…he strikes me as a penguin who speaks out of both sides of his beak."

Nok was glad to find that Trarck's instincts mirrored his own. "I would go as far as to say he speaks out of both his beak and his…" Nok chuckled. "So…is there anyone? Someone we can trust with absolute certainty?"

"Lydeck could have promised favors to any member of the Council. I believe we can trust Cosk, Cleyed, Melk, Colonel Kairg, and a few others, but that's as far as I would go. It seems even that Kerl is now supporting him—she would have been a good choice."

Nok had known the answer before it was asked. "What about the newcomer…what's her name again?"

Trarck shifted, noticeably uncomfortable. "She has her own agenda. She appears to have buddied up with Ki-ok, of all penguins."

It was as agitated as Nok had ever seen Trarck, which was saying a lot. Nok decided not to push the subject. "I'll have her assigned to Colonel Kairg's detachment. He's an excellent judge of character." Trarck only nodded, disappointing Nok's hope for a reaction of some sort.

"Sir, as Commander, you could assign an apprentice to him. You would have to do the same to all members of the Council so not to make it obvious. This has been done in the past—when General Treeg first assembled the Ministry. Apprentices could be made to report to the head of the Council."

"I knew there was a reason why I liked you. You're going to make a fine Commander." Nok looked at Trarck with a hint of mischief in his eyes. "And I have just the penguin for the job."

Trarck looked at him sideways. "Who would that be?" he asked.

"Tearsk. Its time he learned some real responsibility. Don't you think?"

Trarck actually laughed out loud. "It's past time, sir. And Tearsk is about as studious as a Kelp Goose. That, Commander, is a great idea."

Nok laughed as well. "For the good of the colony you know?"

"For the good of the colony," Trarck echoed.

The two headed down into the lower reaches feeling much more positive.

CHAPTER 8

At hearing Keerka's call, Leeg and Kicki scampered toward the sound. But they soon realized that they were chasing echoes, and before long the echoes disappeared. After several turns, backtracking and dead ends, they had to admit that they were lost.

Kicki shivered in the dark. "What do we do now?"

Leeg looked around the dark chamber they found themselves in, trying to make out the shapes of the rocks. "Well, I guess we should just sit down and wait."

"Wait for what? The Shadow Warrior?" Kicki went silent for a moment and seemed to stare through Leeg. "We should keep walking."

"No," Leeg said with little confidence. "My mom is coming for us. If we stay in one spot, she'll be able to find us. My dad always says that a moving squid is hard to catch. So we stay still 'til she comes."

"What if the Shadow Warrior comes looking for us too? Maybe being a slippery squid is better," Kicki said.

"She'll be here." He scooted in close to her to reassure his friend, but being close to Kicki made him feel a little safer too. He considered calling out to Keerka, but worried the Shadow Warrior would hear him first.

They fell into silence until youthful impatience got the better of Leeg and he decided to toss caution to the waves and call for his mom. As he took his breath to call he heard a noise coming from somewhere in the darkness. His heart skipped a beat. Kicki stood up, pressing against his back. She had heard it too.

Leeg strained his eyes and ears, trying to search out the cause of the noise. They heard it again, this time more clearly. It was the sound of clawed feet against stone. "Mom?"

The claws stopped.

"Is that you, Mom?" Leeg whispered.

"It's not your mom. It's the Shadow Warrior," Kicki said.

"How would you know?"

"Just trust me, Leeg."

Kicki pressed her body against his so close that he could feel the hammering of her heart against his back. They heard the claws again and Leeg turned to face his friend. "Kicki, remember what I said about the squid?"

"Yeah?"

"Now's the time to be a squid." The two bolted up the path, away from whatever lurked in the darkness.

They ran hard and as fast as young Rockhoppers could, bumping into rocks and falling over unseen obstacles. With each step they took, they could swear they heard the Shadow Warrior taking two. They ran by a passage that seemed a little brighter, but were in too much of a panic to stop and go back. "That was the way out," Kicki gasped.

"Don't stop! Whatever you do, don't stop."

The footfalls grew louder, a cadence of slapping and clicking of pursuing claws. Leeg could almost feel the monster's breath huffing against his back. He stole a glance backward and spotted the dark form as it crossed the brighter passage. "Go, go, go!" They came to a crossroads and Leeg stuttered, uncertain as to which way to go. Kicki began toward the left, but Leeg led her the other way. They took no more than a few steps before they were greeted with a dead end. "The other way."

"You think?" Kicki said.

They came back to the junction and Leeg braved another glance down the path. The Shadow Warrior moved slow and methodically, no longer running—a shadow against the shadows. Kicki screamed, and Leeg shouted as loud as he could, "Mom!"

In the distance, somewhere in the dark, they heard his mother's call bounce off the stone in reply. "Leeg?"

The Shadow Warrior stopped moving, blending with the darkness so well that Leeg had to wonder if he had seen anything at all. Both Leeg and Kicki called out once more. They heard Keerka's voice and the calls of several Rockhoppers.

The Shadow Warrior had gone silent, and just when Leeg began to think it was standing right in front of them, he heard the scuffling of its feet as it fled. He looked toward Kicki and let out a sigh of relief. "That was too close."

"It could have been worse if we didn't call to your mother," Kicki said after a moment of silence. "Much worse."

When Keerka appeared in the passage, Leeg and Kicki ran to her, chattering and jumbling words about Shadow Warriors and getting lost. "All right, All right. Just settle down. You're safe now," Keerka soothed.

"We're not safe, mom! There's a Shadow Warrior here. It's real!"

Keerka looked at Leeg as she led them into a tunnel with slightly more light. She looked around and spotted Tearsk edging his way toward the back of the group. "Tearsk. You see what your stories have done? The Commander and I are going to find a special punishment for you when we get back."

Tearsk swallowed hard. "Yes, ma'am."

"But Miss Keerka, it's true. He was just here. He was after us," Kicki chimed in.

Keerka gathered the penguins close enough to feel their rapidly beating hearts. "Okay, okay. The dark can play tricks on big imaginations."

"Mom, it's here. We saw it."

Keerka looked toward her squad and relented. "All right. Everybody spread out and see if you can find anything unusual." She turned her attention back to the youths. "If there's anything down here, they'll find it. Now let's get you two home."

CHAPTER 9

The trio spent most of the return trip to the proper end of the warrens in silence. They met up with Nok and Trarck along the way, and Keerka explained the little one's fear. They decided that they weren't in need of further punishment. Keerka saw Kicki safely to her parents and Nok took Leeg back to their nesting spot.

"Dad, we did exactly what you said. We were like a squid, moving as fast as we could to get away from the Shadow Warrior," Leeg said between gulps of nourishment.

"Leeg, I'm sure whatever scared you wasn't a Shadow Warrior. If anything, it was probably a cat. They've been seen on the island before."

"But we *saw* it twice. Once in the cave of Mahak-chig-rantoo, and then again when it was chasing us. What's a cat?"

"A cat is four-legged terror. And if there is one here, then we have a real problem. But son, the cave of Mahak-chig-rantoo is just a story. There's no such thing. And I seriously doubt that a Shadow Warrior has been hiding in the warrens for all this time. It's been a long time since they were last here."

"There is a cave, Dad. There's a hole in the wall that leads to the sea. Kicki and I both saw it. And the Shadow was talking to a Rockhopper."

"Leeg, we don't need any more stories—"

"It's not a story, Dad. Please believe me. I'm not playing make-believe."

Nok looked in his son's eyes. They shone with fear and truth. Nok relented. "All right, son. If what you're saying is true, who was the Rockhopper? You've been around the warrens enough to recognize most of the voices."

"I don't know for sure. I've heard it before, but I was scared and worried about Kicki. If I hear it again, I'll know. I promise you that I'm telling the truth." Leeg leaned his head back, yawning, and his eyelids began to droop.

"You're safe now. After what happened to the Shadow Warriors the last time they were here, I doubt they'd try coming back. Go to sleep and we'll talk again when you wake." Nok escorted Leeg to the nest, and the exhausted fledgling was asleep before Nok turned away.

Keerka walked in and looked at both Nok and Leeg. "How is he?"

"Worn out, scared, but otherwise no worse for the wear."

Keerka nuzzled Leeg to make sure he was asleep. "What do you make of their stories?"

Nok hesitated. Keerka had nearly been killed by Shadow Warriors when General Diutes had come to put the Rockhoppers back in line several months prior. "He said he heard a Rockhopper talking, but he didn't know who. But really, after what the Royals attempted to do here and all of the harm they caused, I would be very surprised if one of us was in collusion with them."

"Kicki doesn't know who the voice belonged to either, but I think we should look into it. They might be telling the truth."

Nok looked at his mate and let out a heavy sigh. "I'll assign a quiet investigation team tomorrow. If what they are saying is true, and if Lydeck finds out, it might be enough for him to convince the Council to recall the vote."

"You're a stronger leader than you think you are," Keerka said.

"Whether I am or not might be irrelevant." Nok turned away and sat next to Leeg.

"If you won't trust yourself, then trust me. You have strong allies, and those allies don't give their faith easily. You're the Commander of the Colony; don't forget that," Keerka said, joining Nok in the nest.

Nok nestled his beak against hers. "That's a stone I'd like to pass to the next chump."

Keerka raised her head. "Are you saying you want to resign?"

"It's tempting. But only if I can find a viable candidate."

"Have you looked for one?"

"I will soon. I think it's time to move away from being a commander."

"So *after* our son is nearly fledged, you decide to quit? Not when we needed to make constant feeding runs and nest changes."

"Hey you could become Commander and oversee legislation involving territorial latrine disputes as well the other exciting measures brought before the Council."

"Nah, I'm not into fair and equal voting. I'm more of a dictator," said Keerka.

"You sure got that right." Nok ducked out of the way of a playful slap. "See what I mean? I get out of line and I'm given lashes."

"If I wasn't so tired I'd give you more." Keerka flopped to her stomach and fell asleep within seconds.

Nok watched his family as they slept and tried to keep the chill of fear away from his heart. If there were Shadow Warriors here, they would have to be dealt with. But first, he had to find out if they *were* here.

CHAPTER 10

Nok had already contacted Trarck before the sun had risen and talked to him about gathering the most trusted and capable Rockhoppers for his 'quiet investigation'.

"Who can we trust? Colonel Kairg and a few others," Trarck said.

Who *could* they trust? That was the question of the day for two days now. The question in itself told Nok all he needed to know. He wasn't Treeg. Under the venerable general's leadership, the Rockhoppers had found solidarity. But now, less than a year since his adoptive father's death, that solidarity had crumbled. The old ways of bickering had returned. He knew Keerka was right: he had plenty of supporters, but the opposition had done everything it could to undermine his leadership. Everything seemed to be unraveling at such speed that he doubted his own resolve. "It's a shame that you even have to ask that question, Trarck. I'm not leaving much of a legacy, am I? When you become Commander, things will be better."

Trarck blinked, confused by Nok's statement. "I'm sure when your time as Commander is over the Rockhoppers will see what you have done. It's just a squall. You can't expect to have calm seas all of the time."

"We've been caught in a storm for some time, and it's given me time to think. After this is all over, I'm going to nominate you as Commander." Trarck began to protest, but Nok cut him off. "You've proven yourself time and again to be a very capable Rockhopper. I'm sure I will have the support of the Council."

Trarck shook his head to the idea. "To be honest, sir, I really don't want the job. I prefer to be in the background, helping out and doing what I can."

"Trarck, you have to trust me…trust my judgment. I've seen the way you handle the Council when they get out of line, and my presence there is a distraction. Lydeck and a few others have seen to that. And your loyal service cannot be discounted by anybody. There are those that think I only achieved my position because of Treeg."

"And there will be those who think the same thing of me. I've been your assistant since you became Commander and before the war, if you remember."

"Of course I do. I'll have to resign before you can get nominated—that might get tricky." Nok looked down a corridor, seemingly lost in thought. "In the meantime, assemble the team. We need to find out if there are any breaches in our defenses. While I doubt there really is a Shadow Warrior hiding down there, I am certain that the little ones saw something. And if there is another way in, then we might be able to use it as an alternate route to go on hunting runs."

"Very well, Commander. I have a few Rockhoppers in mind for this, but I'll have to get them before they go on the scouting run," Trarck said. He began to walk away, but turned back to Nok. "We'll discuss this commander thing later."

Nok let out a laugh. "Of course we will. But right now, I have to gather Tearsk and a few others to inform them of their assignments. I'll see you back in the Council chamber."

CHAPTER 11

"What kind of parade is this?" Packt asked as Nok entered the Council chamber with a line of adolescent penguins in tow. "The young ones are not allowed in here, Commander."

"Precisely, Packt. And that is changing as of today," Nok said, giving the corpulent old matriarch a look which told her he was up to something.

"Very well, Commander Nok," she nodded. "Perhaps you will enlighten the Council when they finally arrive. I swear, what has it come to when the oldest member of the Council arrives before all of the others?" Packt waddled off, continuing to grumble.

The remainder of the Council filtered in with its usual raucousness, but as each member spotted the group of young Rockhoppers standing in front of Nok's station, the noisy rabble turned to grunting murmurs. The murmurs turned to whispers and then to silence when they took their places.

Nok surveyed the chamber happily. He felt a presence at his back and found Trarck, who nodded. Trarck was about to call the meeting to order when Lydeck came rushing in.

"Good of you to join us, Lydeck," Packt said.

Lydeck glared up at her as he took his place at the bottom and right of center. "Yes, Packt. It is good to join you. Forgive my tardiness, but being as how the Commander was otherwise preoccupied, it seemed to me that at least one member of the Council should be present when the scouting team left."

"I didn't know that you were a member of the military. The last I remember, you wanted to avoid that type of service. But if you would like to be, I'm sure that Commander Nok would be able to find a job for you to perform," Packt said, looking at Nok.

"Is that true, Lydeck?" Nok asked. "You've always been so keen to take the fight to the enemy; perhaps you're finally willing to do it personally?"

Lydeck looked around the room as a chorus of Rockhopper jibber reverberated off of the stone walls, either supporting or decrying Nok's offer to Lydeck. His eyes locked on Nok's. "Thank you, Commander. But for the time being, I believe my abilities are best suited for my duties on the Council. Perhaps in the future."

After the calls quieted, the meeting was called to order with the usual pomp and recitations. The young Rockhoppers standing nervous and silent jerked when Nok began to speak. "As I'm sure you are all aware, the scouting team has left to investigate the human vessels. I have every faith in Colonel Kairg's ability to lead the Rockhopper's and keep them out of harm's way," Nok said, looking at Lydeck, who returned the look with a disinterested stare. "He has personally assured me that the task will be completed by midday, at which point we will reconvene to discuss which course of action is best for us. However, in the meantime, I have decided to implement a new program, designed to give the next generation of leaders a head start in the workings of the Council."

Lydeck swiveled his head, looking for objections. "This is not the time for training our youth in the tools of politics. We are at a crosscurrent. One move, one decision, could easily change our course. Perhaps after the threat of the humans has been dealt with would be a better time to implement this policy."

"I believe that there is no better time than the present. This is the perfect situation for the youth. We are resolving a crisis, Lydeck. Our apprentices will learn much. Who knows? Maybe they might even offer a fresh idea," Nok said.

"Members of the Council," Lydeck said as he outstretched his flippers. "Am I the only one among us who thinks that now is not the time? Who sees reason? We have many problems that need to be resolved, and this is an unneeded distraction."

"On the contrary, Lydeck. This idea is genius. We need strong leadership in the future and what better way to achieve that than to have our youth molded into Rockhoppers we can be proud of?" said Kank, a burly old male whose girth was surpassed only by Packt's.

"Thank you, Kank," Nok said. "There is more, however. Each member of the Council will be a mentor to the youth assigned to him or her. You will not only guide them while in the Council, but in their daily lives as well so that they know how to carry themselves in public. Now, before anybody objects by saying that is the job of their parents, I have already spoken to their parents and they are in agreement. With the exception of myself, I don't think anybody on the council had an offspring this season. Am I correct?"

Trasik-lon looked across the chamber to Kerl, who shook her head. "No Commander," Trasik-lon said, somewhat disappointed. "Not this season."

"Very well then," said Nok. He chuckled inwardly. "If there are no further objections, we will get the assignments."

"I still object," Lydeck said. "I suppose the interns are to report to you on what they have learned? This seems to be a convenient way to spy on potential rivals."

"Spy? What reason would I have to spy on any member of the Council?" Nok asked. "It's no secret who wants to replace me as Commander, Lydeck. But, I assure you this has nothing to do with espionage. If it will make you feel better, I will make it a motion and put it to vote."

"Very well, make the motion."

Trarck stepped forward. "A motion has been made. Is there a second?"

"I second the motion," Trasik-lon said, surprising the others.

"Question?" Trarck asked.

"Question," stated Packt.

"Question has been called. Those in favor say aye. Those against say nay."

The calls came at once and when the noise quieted, the votes were counted. "Six in favor, four against with one abstaining. The ayes have it, the motion has been carried," Trarck announced.

"Very good," Nok said. "With the motion, carried I call the meeting to recess to be reconvened after the surveillance team returns. Will the members of the Council please come forward to receive your assigned apprentices?"

Nok got to the work of assigning each young Rockhopper to their mentors. "Tearsk," Nok said. The nervous penguin approached the Commander. "You will be with Lydeck."

Tearsk's eyes widened. "But sir…"

"There is no protesting your assignment. Be thankful I didn't assign you to Packt," Nok said, which drew a look from the old matriarch.

Lydeck began to leave the chamber before anything else could be said. Nok called him back. "Are you forgetting someone?"

Lydeck glared at the young Rockhopper. He mumbled something beneath his breath. "Come with me then." He stormed out of the chamber, Tearsk trying to keep up.

With Lydeck gone, Packt approached Nok. "I'm not sure what you're up to, but I think I like it."

Nok looked at Trarck. "Just looking to the future, Packt."

∧∧∧

Once outside of the chamber Lydeck turned to Tearsk. "I don't know what the Commander is trying to pull, but let me make this very clear. You will not follow me into my private quarters, nor will I be guiding you along anywhere but within the Council chamber."

Tearsk swallowed hard. "But sir, the…"

"No. There are no buts. You are assigned to me and you will do exactly as I say or I will make every day you spend in my company more miserable than the day before. Do I make myself clear?"

"Y-yes sir," Tearsk stammered.

Lydeck looked the Rockhopper over with disdain. "In fact, if you hadn't caused the fledglings to get lost below, I doubt this would have even come up. This is your fault, and that is a fact I will not let you forget."

Tearsk hung his head.

"Now, make yourself scarce. I have private business to attend to."

"But what about the Commander? Where should I go?"

"I don't care where you go. Go up top and make yourself a target for the humans, for all I care. Just stay away from me. And don't even think about running to tell Nok, because if you do, I guarantee you that you really won't like me."

Tearsk desperately wanted to say that he already didn't like him. Instead, he watched Lydeck leave, happy to be free from his company. With nothing else to do, he walked to a dark corner of the warrens and sat alone.

CHAPTER 12

Lydeck scurried along the darkened passages deep in the warrens. He knew the Shadow Warrior was waiting, but Nok's little show had made him late. But in less than a month's time it wouldn't matter.

Lost in his thoughts, Lydeck almost didn't hear the scouting party coming up the path. His heart began to pound. How would he explain this to the Commander? He looked around and spotted a crevice. The raucous group of penguins were too busy with their discussion of the breach to notice Lydeck bolt across the path. He struggled to squeeze in the narrow opening, just managing to hide his yellow head plume as they passed by.

"Well I don't think even a Shadow Warrior could get through that breach in either high *or* low tide. The surf is just too powerful. Leeg must have seen a cat," one of the Rockhoppers said.

"An overactive imagination," another said.

"We'll report what we know to the commander and leave out the conjecture. Remember, nobody says a word to anybody."

Lydeck strained to hear more, but the Rockhoppers were soon out of earshot. "No secrets," Lydeck muttered to himself as he squeezed out of the crag. He wondered why Nok wanted the group to keep it quiet. And then he realized they were talking about the Shadow Warrior. Now he had no doubt that Nok's son had seen them. Suddenly everything had just become a lot more complicated.

Lydeck entered the cave huffing for breath. He chirped a distinct call to the Shadow Warrior and waited. He was about to call again when he heard the response, a subtle click from the other side of the pool. Lydeck dove in without hesitation and scrambled up the other side.

"Your comrades were here not long ago," the Shadow Warrior accused.

"Yes," Lydeck said. He shifted his feet. "Things have become slightly more complicated."

"How so?"

Lydeck was about to answer when two dark figures emerged from the breach. More Shadow Warriors. Lydeck stared at them and felt himself begin to shake.

The Shadow noticed his gaze. "Pay them no mind. If the group searching the cave had been more thorough, we would have killed them."

Lydeck swallowed hard. "Yes, yes. Of course you would have. We were seen by Commander Nok's son and another."

The Shadow Warrior fixed Lydeck a stare so cold that Lydeck couldn't help but shiver. "Are you certain it was the Commander's son?"

"As much as I can be. They were lost and told stories of a Shadow Warrior. Fortunately, the adults don't believe them."

"Have you been identified?" the Royal hissed. The large penguin took a step forward.

"If I had I wouldn't be here." Lydeck took a step back, keeping watch on the two other Shadows.

The Royal eyed the diminutive Rockhopper for what felt like an eternity. Lydeck's mouth went dry. "This does complicate matters. The messengers are on their way to meet Mearna's scouts as we speak. If you cannot uphold your end of the bargain, then we will have to take the island by force."

"I assure you, I will become Commander. If not by vote, then with the Royal Emperor's backing. You will not have to use deadly force."

The Shadow Warrior remained silent for another moment. "Nok will have to be taken out of the equation, one way or another."

Lydeck scratched his claws on the rock nervously. He doubted that he had the ability to kill Nok. Nok was a well-seasoned warrior; he had helped kill Liutites. Lydeck had never killed another penguin. He had even hid when Treeg defeated Diutes' company. "I doubt that I can get to him. He is too strong for me. But not for you," he said.

"No," the Shadow said. "It would not be prudent of us. Not with Mearna arriving soon after. There is another way to eliminate the problem of Nok *and* his mate."

"How?"

"Kill his son," the Shadow Warrior said, his eyes glinting.

Lydeck froze. "No," he whispered. "I can't. That's too much."

"You will." The Shadow loomed over him. "You will do it, or we will kill you, and then we will kill the Rockhoppers."

Lydeck struggled to find words. "But he is just a fledgling."

"He is a sacrifice for the greater good—one small penguin for the safety of the entire colony. Once it is done, you will become Commander, and peace will finally come to this island." The Shadow Warrior glared down at Lydeck. "That is what you want? One small act, and you will have everything that you desire. But," the Shadow paused and turned away, "if you lack the fortitude, I will hold true to my promise."

"But, but, it's killing a fledgling," Lydeck said.

"What is your answer?" The two other Shadow Warriors joined him at his side.

Lydeck stared at the ground. Everything would change. Distantly, as if he were watching the events unfold from afar, he felt his head nod. "Yes," he said. Lydeck looked up at the Shadow Warrior. What he saw was Cuasan, devilish king-spirit of the Underworld. His fate was sealed. "I'll do it."

The Shadow Warrior nodded. "See to it quickly. Mearna will be here in a moon's cycle." The three departed through the breach, leaving Lydeck alone in the darkness.

CHAPTER 13

Nok and Keerka stood on the rocky hill above the Rockhopper haven, escaping the chattering echoes of the colony below. It was on this spot that General Treeg had witnessed the destruction of the Caracara; the ship that had brought the poachers who killed the general's last surviving offspring Cort. From this vantage point, Nok and Keerka could see three boats anchored out beyond the swells. More killers were coming ashore for another day's target practice.

Nok watched them, silently hoping for a wave to upturn their boats. He resisted the urge to call the Rockhoppers to battle. Their numbers were too small. The colony had been decimated, and there were no allies to call on for help. He looked to Keerka, who had both anger and worry in her eyes. "Do you believe in fate?" he asked.

Keerka remained silent for a few moments as she watched the small boats trudge their way toward the island. "Fate is what we make it, Nok. The decisions we make determine our future. Belief in fate or destiny only serves to absolve us of the accountability of our choices."

Nok stared at his mate. "I was speaking with Packt."

"Packt is a good penguin," Keerka said. "She's been around longer than most other penguins, and not just here."

"True. I always thought she didn't care for me too much."

"I think everybody thinks that unless you take the time to know her."

"True again. But during our talk, she started talking about that ridiculous myth about the penguin who will lead us to peace. I didn't want to argue about it, but she said something that made me think."

"The old bird can do that."

"Yes she can. She talked about the prophecy and implied each clan has to choose their leader, the one who will lead them to that place. Maybe we all have a place. And she said fortuitous events will come soon. I have no idea what she's talking about. Whether she thinks she's a prophet or if her mind is becoming addled with age I'm not sure. But I've been thinking about what she said about choosing our leader. And I've made that choice." Nok waited for a reply. "I think Trarck is the Rockhopper we need to lead the colony."

Keerka stared at Nok, let out a heavy breath. "Nok," she started to say.

"I know, I know. You believe in me and think I'm the one who is best suited to lead us." Nok turned away.

"No, Nok."

"No?"

"I do believe in you. That's why I think you have made the right choice. We've been through enough. However brief it has been, I think it's time to pass the stone to the next Rockhopper. Trarck is well suited for the job."

"You think this is best? Really?"

"Yes. I'll admit that some of it is out of selfish reasons. I can't wait for us to have time for our family. Trarck is seen as more neutral to the Rockhoppers, and there would be no calls of nepotism or bias at him becoming Commander. It's the right decision. I'm happy."

"Thank you, Keerka. I couldn't have done any of this without you. You seem to know everything—so much more than me, and always what's best."

"You just remember that the next time I ask you to clean the nest."

Nok laughed and was about to remind her that he was still the Commander when the roar of distant jet engines caught his attention. The pair stiffened at the sound. They were about to make a dash for cover, but the jets were already flying low over the island. Instead, they ran to the edge of the cliff and looked for a ledge to hop down.

They cringed more when they heard the barely audible sound of gunfire. They looked at the boats, guessing that the humans had spotted them and were taking their shots. They were confused by what they saw. The Argentinean gunmen on the boats were firing at the British warplanes. The sleek, delta-winged fighters peeled away and quickly disappeared into the horizon.

"That was unexpected," Nok said as they got out of sight.

"As is that," Keerka said, pointing her beak toward sea. "The little boats are headed back to the big ones."

Nok and Keerka stared at the activities in puzzlement. They watched as two zodiacs hooked up to the boats and the men scrambled back on board. The third boat, a larger skiff, lagged behind, motoring in circles as it waited its turn to dock. "What are they doing? Are they leaving?" Nok asked. Keerka could only shrug. They heard the distant sound of the RAF fighter's engines screaming back in their direction.

Nok spotted the familiar contrails of a missile launch and the two Rockhoppers stood transfixed by the distant spectacle. There was no place to run or hide from the projectiles. The third boat gave up on docking and sped away, back toward the shore. They watched the distant vapor trails of the missiles appear and in a blink, the anchored ships erupted into balls of flame.

Nok and Keerka stood in awe, perplexed by what they had witnessed. Having only encountered missiles directed at them, they had never had the chance to appreciate their destructive power. Their awe soon turned to worry when they realized the jets were still headed in their direction. They closed their eyes and huddled together waiting for the blast that would send them to join so many other Rockhoppers in The Great Sea.

The roar of supersonic engines passed them by. Keerka opened her eyes and scanned the sky. "Nothing," she said. "They didn't attack."

Nok opened his eyes and looked around, wary of a stray missile headed their way. He looked at Keerka and laughed. "You're right. They didn't attack! Why are they attacking each other? Does this mean we have allies among them?"

Keerka had to laugh. "Ever the hopeful one, aren't you? I doubt it. Remember the stories of the human war that took place long ago? It appears as if they're at it again."

Nok didn't let it dampen his mood. "Well, the enemy of our enemy—"

"Is still our enemy," Keerka interrupted.

Nok nodded. "Right. There's still one boat out there. I'm sure we can handle that. Let's get below. Make sure Leeg is safe and meet me at the western shore; I'm calling for the attack. This is the break we needed."

When they reached passage to the Warrens Nok stopped and faced Keerka. "Fortuitous events indeed. That frumpy old penguin was right. When I see her, I'm going to give her the biggest beak nuzzle she's ever gotten."

Keerka gave Nok a wry look. "If you think I'll be jealous, I won't. In fact, I'm a little scared for you."

They hurried below.

CHAPTER 14

The Warrens were a frenzy of activity. Rockhoppers hurried about the stone walkways shouting and taking orders. Lydeck took advantage of the chaos and ducked in and out of shadows. He made his way toward the crèche where he was sure to find Leeg. He spotted the youngsters standing in the passageway to the care center, watching the turmoil.

"Lydeck," a voice called. "What are you doing? You will have some explaining to do to Commander Nok."

It was Trasik-lon, the strong up-and-comer on the Council. "I was just…just about to see to the safety of the—"

"Never mind that; there are others who oversee safety. Where is Tearsk? Why are you purposely defying the Council?"

"I haven't defied anyone. You know as well as I that Commander Nok implemented this program to keep watch on his adversaries. It was a show of power. That's all. And I have no intention of playing his game."

Trasik-lon took a step back. "Settle yourself. You have my backing, but only when the time is right. Your outburst in the Council has cost you support. The older members want to see an even-keeled commander, not a penguin who loses control when he doesn't get his way."

"I did not lose control," Lydeck said in an even tone, trying to mask his impatience. "I was simply astounded by how quickly the Council agreed to the program. And trust me, with or without the support of the elder members, I will be Commander."

"You won't be if you continue to agitate the Council. Speaking of which, we're going to shore to see the warriors off to battle. It would be proper if you would join us." Trasik-lon turned to leave.

"I have to take care of something first. I will be there for their return."

"If that is your choice. A commander shows not only ambition, but leadership as well."

Lydeck huffed away. "When I command the colony I won't suffer the likes of Trasik-lon. I'll purge the Council of those who disagree." He looked back to the crèche. Leeg and his friend were gone. He uttered a quiet curse and walked by the entry to see if he could spot them, but the shadows within the small cavern made it difficult.

Lydeck continued past the crèche. He had to think of someway to lure Leeg away. With both Nok and Keerka distracted by the impending attack, it would be the perfect time. He hovered around the dark spaces of the corridor, waiting for his opportunity. His patience was rewarded when both Leeg and Kicki stepped back into the corridor. Lydeck took a breath and began to walk with caution toward the pair.

"Lydeck," an angry voice called from the other end of the corridor.

"This has got to be a joke," Lydeck muttered. It was Tearsk's parents. "What can I do for you?" Lydeck said in his best political voice.

"What have you done to our son? It was a proud day for him to have been chosen to be apprenticed on the Council, and he had the bad luck of being assigned to you. The poor thing is just sitting by the nest, heartbroken and dejected. Well, what have you got to say for yourself and your inexcusable behavior?"

"Rokuk…it is Rokuk, isn't it?"

"You know my name as well as any other's," Rokuk said, puffing his chest. He was a robust Rockhopper, with nearly twice Lydeck's girth.

"Now is hardly the time to discuss personal matters. If you haven't noticed, we are in a state of emergency. Now if you will excuse me, I have pressing business to take care of." Lydeck tried to step around the angry father, who pushed him back with his stout frame.

"There is no time like the present. I want an answer, and I want it now."

Lydeck glared at Rokuk. "Very well, then. Your son is a spoiled, incapable waste of my time. He is better suited for baiting seals than being on the Council. In fact, you and your crest-less mate should be sitting on your nest, commiserating on how you raised such a hapless, ignorant, waste of feather and bone. Although judging by the looks of his parents, your answer is no further than the tip of your beak. Now excuse me." He tried to leave, but Rokuk blocked his path once again.

"How dare you say such things about my son! Nok should have left you to die on that ship. And to think I risked my life for your rescue. You mark my words, you loathsome heap of guano, I'll see you removed from the Council. How such a spineless Skua like you made it on the Council is beyond me."

"Most things *are* beyond you, Rokuk." Lydeck stepped around the huffing Rockhopper, hiding his fear. He breathed a sigh of relief when he heard the couple's angry chatter fade down the corridor. "Now to take care of what needs to be done."

CHAPTER 15

Leeg and Kicki stood as close to the entrance as possible without breaking the crèche minder's continuously repeated rule of not going into the corridor.

"Do you think your father will lead the Rockhoppers into battle?" asked Kicki.

"I don't know. I don't think he does that anymore. He just yells at the Council now." Leeg listened to a shrill call reverberate off of the stone walls.

"Well, maybe he'll yell at the humans," Kicki joked.

"Did you hear that? The Rockhoppers are attacking the humans. That was my father. He just called the warriors to battle." He looked back at Kicki. Her eyes were closed, her head swaying back and forth. "Why do you keep doing that?"

Kicki's eyes shot open. She stared at Leeg, not saying a word.

"Are you all right?" Thinking his friend was ill, Leeg was about to get the crèche minder, but Kicki stopped him.

"You're in danger. A Rockhopper. The sea. The rocks. The cave."

"What are you talking about, Kicki?"

"Leeg," said Lydeck when he approached the distracted youth. "Where are your parents?"

Leeg stiffened. He recognized the Rockhopper who was talking to the Shadow Warrior.

"What's wrong? Gull got your tongue? Speak when your elders address you."

"I don't know, sir," Leeg answered in a quiet voice.

"Speak up. I can't hear you through all of this ruckus."

Leeg swallowed hard, his mouth dry. "I don't know, sir."

"Well then, what do you say we go find them?"

Leeg watched Lydeck. "I don't know, sir. I think we should wait in the crèche."

"Nonsense, young one. If your parents are otherwise occupied, you should be taken to a safe place before the attack comes."

"The attack?" Leeg said, even more alarmed. "What attack? I thought my father called to attack them."

"And if the humans break through our defenses? What then? We have to get you to someplace safe. Now, come along."

"I think I should wait for my parents here."

"No. You're coming with me."

Wide-eyed and fearful, Leeg stared at Lydeck, but didn't move.

"Now," Lydeck said. "We haven't much time."

Leeg took a reluctant step forward and Kicki stepped in. "If he's going then I'm going."

Lydeck glared at her. "This is not for you. Leeg is the Commander's son; we have protocols to follow."

"I don't care about protocols. I'm going, and that's that." She stood her ground.

Lydeck appeared to be trying to keep his irritation under control, and seemed about to lose it when Leeg chimed in.

"No, Kicki," Leeg said. "You have to stay here." She tried to argue, but Leeg stopped her. "Just trust me, you *have* to." Leeg looked into her eyes to make sure she understood what he was doing. She had to tell the others who he went with and where. "I'm sure I'll be safe. He's a member of the Council; I have to obey him."

Her eyes fluttered as if she were about to pass out. "All right, I'll wait right here," she said, nodding to Leeg.

Lydeck looked between the two of them, not picking up on the exchange. "Come on then. Let's go. This way," he said, ushering him toward a side passage.

Leeg hurried alongside of Lydeck, looking back to Kicki.

^^^

Kicki paced near the entrance of the crèche, ignoring the new minder's frequent requests to move away from the opening. Only a minute had passed since Leeg had left, and she fought against the urge to follow them. She ran to the crèche minder instead. "You have to call the Commander."

"I'm sure he's very busy right now," Eeco, an old, sterile female who had jumped at the chance to watch over the little ones answered.

"But Leeg is gone. He took him."

The crèche minder stood in alarm. Her first day on the job, and she had already lost one. "Who took him? Where did he go?" She looked around the room, trying to spot Leeg.

"Lydeck did. He was the one talking to the Shadow Warrior. I'm afraid he's going to hurt him."

The minder relaxed and sat back. "The Shadow Warrior? I know you're scared, my little rock-cress, but those are just stories. I assure you—"

"They aren't stories. I saw one. Leeg is in danger." Kicki huffed and waved her flippers.

"That's enough of that. Lydeck is a member of the Council, I'm sure he has his reasons. Now you go sit next to the wall. We don't need you frightening the others with your stories."

Kicki growled as she was led to the far end of the cavern. She had to find a way out to at least tell Keerka.

CHAPTER 16

Commander Nok walked along the edge of a rocky cove, where a natural breakwater kept the raging Atlantic at bay on most days. Kelp gulls squawked while flying against a powder blue sky, the first tendrils of fog threatening to encompass the island. The first wave of attack, led by Colonel Kairg, stood poised and ready to begin the strike on the colonel's command.

"Are you sure you don't want to join us, Commander? It will be another etching on the stone of victory," Kairg asked. "Come on, Commander. We haven't fought side by side since that debacle at the Falklands."

Nok felt the old familiar sensation, a rush of excitement mixed with a nauseating fear as the battle grew near. He was surprised to feel the temptation of taking the fight to the enemy once again. "I actually would like to, Colonel. But, as Commander, I regretfully can't. I have to lead from the rear and all of that nonsense. Besides, Keerka would have a feather from my crest if she found out I went without her," he said, adding the last thought in a quiet voice.

"Ah, she's got ahold of your tail feathers that tight, does she?"

Nok gave Kairg a look of resigned agreement.

"Well then, Commander. I will see you when our work is done."

"The second and third waves will be right behind. Remember, Colonel— you must get them before they reach the beach. We will be in for a much harder time if they get their feet on the ground."

"No worries about that, sir. We'll get them in the water. We've done this work before." Kairg saluted and ran to his squad of twenty Rockhoppers.

Nok watched until each group had disappeared into the waves. Staring at the sea, he felt Sergeant Trarck come up behind him. "By the Ancients, Trarck, I hope this attack is a success. Lydeck will have a field day if we fail."

Trarck came to Nok's side. "Colonel Kairg is quite capable, Commander. He picked the squads himself. He chose Tretak to join them as well."

Nok looked at Trarck, who quickly looked away. "I'm sure she'll be fine."

Trarck ignored the comment. "Most of these Rockhoppers took part in the attacks against the boats during our first success against the humans. They'll do what is necessary."

"I know they will. Kairg is one of the strongest and most experienced warriors among us. But there's a lot riding on this."

"I think, sometimes you worry too much, my friend."

"And sometimes not enough." Nok studied the sea and watched the incoming fog. "Trarck, tell Lieutenant Ki-ok to take the reserve squad to the flat beach and wait there. If the men somehow get past Kairg's squads, Ki-ok's forces are to attack the boat in the surf, where the men will be most vulnerable."

"Lieutenant Ki-ok, sir? Are you sure that is wise? Not many Rockhoppers have much faith in him."

"He'll do fine. He just needs a confidence boost. Besides, I doubt the men will get past Colonel Kairg."

"Yes, sir." Trarck turned toward the warrens, but hesitated when Nok didn't join him. "Are you coming, Commander?"

Nok stared at the waves. It had been so long since the colony had seemed anything close to normal. "No, Sergeant. I'm going to ride the crests and watch the battle."

"Are you sure that's safe, Nok?"

"I'm never certain of anything." Nok watched the waves crash against the rocks, timing his leap. "Station scouts along the shore between here and the beach. If it all goes wrong, we'll need to know as quickly as possible. Be prepared for anything and make certain the reserves are at full readiness." Nok dove into the retreating surf without another word.

He let the tide pull him away from the shore and dove under the rolling waves, swimming two hundred meters away from the coast. The South Atlantic proved kind enough to produce large swells. Nok swam to the crest of each swell and looked toward the west, hoping to catch sight of the boat. He had no fear of a Phocid swimming under him to make him a meal. The poachers had killed the last of them just before the war.

Riding the surf, he felt reinvigorated. It had been too long since he had been to sea. With his duties as Commander, the burden of gathering and feeding Leeg had fallen almost entirely on Keerka's shoulders. Nok vowed to change that as soon as he relinquished command to Trarck. The more thought he put into it, the more he understood why some members of the Council might have doubted his leadership and lost patience. Rockhoppers belonged in the sea, not crowded and kept in the caves. "If I hadn't waited, the fortuitous events would have never transpired and more would have died. I did well." Nok tried to convince himself that he *was* a good leader; that he measured up to Treeg.

A twinge of bitterness toward Treeg rose within him. The venerable General Treeg had left his legacy, and Nok decided he would leave his. Not by matching his predecessor, but by no longer trying to.

Nok rode to the top of another swell and spotted the boat motoring its way toward the shore. He realized that he was not only jeopardizing his own safety, but if he were to be seen, it could very well take away Kairg's element of surprise. He dove below and swam back to the rocks, his mind clearer. Lydeck and his followers be damned, he would bring unity back to the colony.

CHAPTER 17

Colonel Kairg and his squad rested on the surface, hiding among the floating beds of kelp. Each member of the squad were spaced out just enough to get a good view of the approaching boat. Like Commander Nok, they rode the swells, using the rise as a vantage point. Their rest was brief; the skiff, barely seaworthy, motored its way around a sea stack, slapping through each wave. The occupants clutched the sides, hoping not to be tossed into the icy water.

Colonel Kairg called the Rockhoppers to action. The squad answered back with braying calls and dove below the surface. The tide tugged and pushed at the Rockhoppers. They tried to muster the speed necessary to clear the sides of the skiff, angling ahead, hoping to intercept the moving target with a precise leap.

The penguins flapped hard as they approached, willing their wings to give them a final push needed to clear the waves. They looked to the surface of the churning sea and spotted the shadow of the skiff bouncing along the water. One hard beat of flippers, and the squad of seven Rockhoppers sprung from waves.

The first Rockhopper aboard was Tretak. She tumbled into the boat and tried to get her footing on the crowded, wet, rocking deck. She looked up in time to see five of the Rockhoppers soar over the boat, missing it entirely; the sixth hit the driver and caromed into the sea.

"This isn't good," she said. The lone Rockhopper looked from man to man as they shouted panicked and indecipherable words, pointing at her. The pitching of the boat made getting to the side to escape nearly impossible. She stood and promptly fell back into the sloshing pool filling the bottom of the boat. The men kept yelling at the driver. The driver pointed at her and clutched the edge again for safety.

More jostling threw Tretak against a man's legs. She stared in horror as the wide-eyed man stared back. More shouting came from the driver. The man looked to the driver, then back at the Rockhopper. She saw the man's eyes dart between her and the pilot. He raised his hand but pulled back, as if he were afraid to touch her. The other men yelled louder and he shouted back. The man loosened his grip on the wood bench and reached for her. There was nothing she could do. She tried to bite him, but he lifted her by the foot and flung her away. In the brief moment of spinning flight, she glimpsed several Rockhoppers leaping from the waves toward the boat. Her body slapped hard against the water and she stayed there, dazed but relieved to be alive.

"I've never actually seen a Rockhopper fly," Colonel Kairg said to Tretak when he came to check on her.

"It wasn't my intention to fly, sir," she said, trying to shake off the shock of the encounter.

"Can you continue or do you need to go to shore? The others need our help."

Tretak puffed her chest and scowled, indignant. "I'm right behind you, sir."

Kairg, followed closely by Tretak, approached the skiff and found it going in circles, slapping on waves. What remained of the crew clung to the skiff's dilapidated wood sides for life. The second wave of Rockhoppers who had managed to make it aboard were tossed from the boat by either man or motion as quickly as they arrived. The plan was falling apart. With no other recourse, Kairg called off the attack.

"We can still take them, sir," said Tretak. "There are only three left."

"We'll take care of them in the shallows, if the sea doesn't take them first." As if to emphasize the latter, the two heard the shouts of a man calling to his companions as he desperately tried to keep his head above water. Kairg looked to Tretak. "Take half of the group and drown that man. I'll take the others and follow their vessel to shore."

"Are you certain, Colonel? I've never actually led an attack."

"Are you questioning your commander's judgment, Tretak?"

Tretak stiffened. "No, sir. Not at all, sir."

"You have as much fight as any of us. You'll do fine. Carry out the task successfully and I'll see that you get a proper rank."

Tretak's eyes widened. "Yessir." She swam away, calling out for members of her squad.

Tretak's group amassed thirty meters away from the haplessly splashing and yelling man. "Our orders are to put an end to that human's noise and rejoin Colonel Kairg near the shore. As per the colonel's orders, I will lead the group. We will grab the human by its loose outer skin and pull it to the seafloor. They can't hold their air like we can, so it should only take a moment. However, be mindful of its hind legs—even though they're weak swimmers, they have a good kick."

Tretak dove beneath the surface. The squad followed her closely and circled below the man. She saw that his kicks were sluggish, the effort to keep his head above the frigid water was proving too much for the man.

The squad continued to circle, waiting on Tretak's signal to attack. When she saw the man's head dip below the water, she gave the signal. The Rockhoppers moved in swiftly, and taking ahold of loose clothing in their beaks, the group began to dive. Like a team of oarsmen, each penguin's flipper thrust in unison with the others. The current tugged and pulled at the team, and the man thrashed wildly.

Two Rockhoppers were kicked away but were replaced by two more. Despite their best efforts, the man's fight was proving to be too much and the penguins began to lose their grip. Tretak circled around, watching and guiding her compatriots. The man succeeded in breaking free of all but three of his would-be killers and began kicking toward the surface. Tretak's eye caught the shadow of the skiff as it passed overhead. If the man surfaced now, he might be rescued, and she wouldn't allow that. Two meters more and the man would break the surface. She had to think of a way; something to even the odds.

The answer smacked Tretak in the face like the tail of a Sea Trout. "Why not just attack it?" There was no time to inform the others of her plan. She circled the man once more to gain momentum and pointed her beak at where she thought the man's throat would be. The attack would have to be perfectly timed; if she missed her target and hit its hard skull, things could get worse.

Tretak gave a final thrust of her flippers. Seeing her target, she closed her eyes just before impact. She felt the soft neck give way beneath her beak and heard the man's muffled underwater scream, followed by bubbles of air popping around her. The man convulsed in a final desperate act to swim to the surface. She opened her eyes to see wispy billows of blood float away with the current.

Satisfied that her task had been done, Tretak allowed herself to float away. It was time to help the colonel. She pulled her flippers up to swim but was pulled back in an instant by a grip so tight, that even if she wanted to breathe, she would not have been able to. The world swam around her in eddies of fear and confusion. Her body was pulled one direction, then another as her panicked mind struggled to figure out what horrible trap she had been ensnared in. The grip began cut off the blood flow to her brain. She knew she had to get free soon; if she lost consciousness, her body's reflex to breath would kick in and she would drown. What an embarrassing way for a penguin to die, she thought. Her body thrashed through the water, and she saw the source of her torment. The human clutched her neck.

The yanking about ceased, but the grip didn't ease. They were falling toward the seafloor; the man was dying, but not quickly enough. Her graying vision began to grow dimmer as she began to lose consciousness. She paddled and kicked in desperation but could not break free. The man's body fell through a sparse grove of kelp and hit the seafloor. They tumbled through fronds of kelp and over sand and stone in a final battle. As her world turned black, she felt the grip slacken. She pulled her flippers through the water and finally broke free. Floating toward the surface, Tretak tried to flap her wings again, but couldn't find the energy. Her momentum came to a stop. She became aware of her body as it drifted back down, and there was nothing she could do except hold her breath, until that too left her.

Tretak's eyes opened when she felt a sharp pinch on her wing, followed by a similar one on the other wing and she began to rise once more. It took a second for her to realize that her vision was returning. Dark, spectral forms floated around her head. She wondered if it was Kraysol, the gatherer of the dead, coming to take her to the Great Sea. The forms became sharper. They were Rockhoppers. Were they the spirits of those who had departed before? A Rockhopper floated before her face, said something, and swam toward the surface. Her mind connected with what she had seen and she realized that she was still alive and she still had air. She flapped her wings away from the Rockhoppers who had them in their beaks and shot upward. "Of course they wouldn't leave," she thought. "Why would I think they would?"

Tretak's head cleared the surface and she took a much needed deep breath. She floated on the sea's angry swells until she got her bearings.

"Are you all right?" A Rockhopper asked.

"Yes. Yes, I'm all right. Thank you for coming for me."

"What else would we do?" the young male asked.

Tretak nodded. "You're right. What else would a decent Rockhopper do? Now, let's catch up with Colonel Kairg and finish this."

CHAPTER 18

Tretak led her squad through the increasingly violent waves. The squad felt like they were being pulled toward shore more than swimming to it. They could all feel the vibration of the skiff's propeller through the water as they moved closer. Their hearts raced in anticipation of the attack. The squad dove below the crest in unison. The corpse of a human tumbled along the ocean floor, the heavy tide buffeting the body, pulling at arms and legs in a tug-of-war between the land and the sea. They ignored it and swam on.

They spotted the skiff moving on a straight course. Tretak saw the shadowy forms of several Rockhoppers as they shot upward to intercept the boat. They disappeared from sight, only to reenter the water after missing their target. It was obvious to Tretak that the tide was playing havoc on the colonel's plan. Whatever humans were on board were going to escape, or at least make it to land. Nothing could be done except watch them escape and see Kairg's, no, *their* mission end in failure.

The breakers pummeled the skiff, the ferocity of the waves slowing its approach. Tretak moved in close enough to see the propeller cutting through the surf. While she didn't know much about human machinery, she knew enough to know that the thing at back was how it swam. If only she could stop it from moving. Frustrated, she began to surface and cursed a bed of kelp for blocking her path. She had seen enough kelp for one day.

Her squad came along side of her as she rested on the water. They watched the skiff rise on a large swell and collectively held their breath, hoping it would capsize and toss the lone occupant overboard. The skiff slapped hard against water, but the human held its grip. Another squad member came along-side of her. "Do you want to make a run at it?"

"Do you think we'll fare any better?"

"Probably not, but it is worth a try." Tretak paddled forward, pushing broken kelp out her way. "It would be a little easier without getting caught up in this accursed weed." Her mind flashed back to the body tumbling amongst the kelp fronds and getting ensnared by the waving forest. She looked at the skiff and then to the other Rockhopper. "Quickly, grab hold of an end of this kelp."

The other looked at her as if she had been eating sand.

"Just do it. I have a plan." Tretak explained her idea. "We'll have to stay in perfect sync. We'll only get one try at this. Now, let's go."

Tretak took her end of the kelp frond and the other took his. They started toward the skiff, each beat of their wings matching the other's perfectly. They dove below and shot up, porpoising above the surface in unison to minimize drag and the pull of the tide. Tretak spotted Colonel Kairg riding a swell, but she had no time to explain—the skiff was near the shallows, and soon the waves would push it ashore.

The pair passed by the skiff close enough to hear the overtaxed engine sputtering and giving its last bit of life to see the boat to shore. They dove and arced back, heading directly for the propeller. The skiff and penguins met in a heartbeat and the two Rockhoppers guided the frond toward the spinning blades. The kelp caught the shaft, and the two penguins crossed over one another to ensure it held. They held the kelp frond tight in their beaks for another crisscross. Tretak felt a juicy snap vibrate through her beak. She saw her partner float away with nearly half of the frond still clenched in his beak.

Tretak clung tightly to the remaining section, swimming out of the boat's meager wake. The surf aided the skiff now; soon the waves would break close enough to shore to pull the boat along. She swam with all of her strength and got underneath the boat, rising and falling with the surf and vessel. She saw kelp loosely wrapped just below the anti-ventilation plate and behind the prop. The tide battered her to and fro, and she felt her strength begin to ebb. She fell back and let the kelp stipe catch the blades. She tried to bring it around for another pass, but the kelp was too rigid, and she was too tired.

Tretak watched the blades come to a satisfying halt. She waited behind the boat and watched as Kairg's Rockhoppers came near. At least they would have easier time of getting on the thing. She was about to swim away and let the others do their work when she saw the kelp snap and the propeller come back to life. A large wave carried the skiff away and into shallows. The crestfallen Tretak let the wave carry her as well.

Tretak surfaced and as she rode the next wave in Colonel Kairg popped up beside her. "That was quite ingenious. It very nearly worked. Now, come on, we'll get the beast in the shallows and we'll talk later."

Tretak watched Kairg swim away letting the push of the wave bolster his speed. She was too embarrassed to tell him she hadn't the strength left to fight.

CHAPTER 19

Lieutenant Ki-ok stood on the rocky shore watching and waiting for the skiff to clear the breakers and enter the shallows. Waves slowly carried the boat in. "This is it," Ki-ok shouted, his voice sounding more like a gull's than the bray of a Rockhopper. "There is only one human remaining, one human. We'll move in and kill it on my command."

The last survivor leapt from the skiff as soon as the keel hit sand. Colonel Kairg's group attacked before he could take his second step and Lieutenant Ki-ok's beak fell open. "What? What is he doing?" he asked Sergeant Kuk-kek, who stood back, watching the display of Rockhopper resolve.

"It looks like they are attacking the human, sir."

"This will not stand…won't stand at all. All squads, attack now. Attack!" Ki-ok stood with feet firmly planted in the sand as his warriors charged past him and ran into the surf.

By the time Ki-ok's Rockhoppers arrived, the colonel's had already seen to the man's demise. The battered corpse rolled in the shallow surf; streams of blood carried on the back of dissipating waves melded with sand and sea. The body rolled to its back and at last became beached on the coarse black sand. Petrels appeared out of the sky, squabbling with gulls over feeding rights.

By the time Colonel Kairg came ashore to inspect the kill, Lieutenant Ki-ok had paced a rut into the beach. He was livid, and when he could take no more, he marched toward his superior. "How dare you, Colonel. How dare you."

Colonel Kairg let out an exaggerated breath. "How dare I, how dare I what, Lieutenant?"

"You know damn well, Colonel. Commander Nok assigned this sector to me to prevent any humans from coming ashore. The Commander assigned *me*."

"There is a human ashore right here, Lieutenant. You have failed your assigned task. Perhaps you should push it back into the sea and kill it again"

Ki-ok met him with a red-eyed stare. "You know what I'm talking about. You know. You're always trying to steal the glory, bask in the praise of the Commander and the Council. Always."

"Lieutenant, I assure you I have no need to bask in anybody's praise. I was simply not informed that this was your sector to protect. But if I may offer some advice for the future," Kairg said, stepping in close to Ki-ok, "perhaps you should move a little quicker and be a little more assertive. That might prevent others from having to do your job in the future."

"Your audacity appalls me, Colonel. It simply appalls me. It is unbefitting of an officer of the ministry. Believe me, Colonel; I promise you I will bring this before the Council...I promise you."

"I doubt that the Council will have the patience to hear you out twice, Lieutenant. They...*we*, still haven't forgotten your cowardice at the Falklands. Had you joined in the attack against the remaining humans, the task would have been completed that much sooner. But you stood on the beach with your reserves, watching, waiting, and when we were attacked—you fled."

"We've been through this, Colonel. We have been through it. Commander Boulet told me to wait until called. We were never called." Ki-ok's voice lowered along with his head. "Never."

"It's called taking initiative, Ki-ok. Many Rockhoppers died because we took too long to finish the task. You may have prevented their deaths."

Kairg turned away.

Ki-ok walked around to face Kairg. "It is not my fault she died. Not my fault. We all obeyed the orders given to us. The deaths of our families are on the Overlord and our own ignorance. Our own *ignorance*. Klytic's death is not my fault…not my fault."

Kairg glared at Ki-ok. "Never mention her name again. You are not worthy to speak it." Kairg began to walk away, speaking without looking back. "Your failure here will be brought to the attention of the Council, as well as your insubordination."

Ki-ok was standing, trembling with a helpless rage, when a voice cut through his thoughts.

"Do you think Kairg has enough influence in the Council to see you stripped of your rank?"

Ki-ok turned to find Tretak standing beside him. He studied her long enough to make her think she had misspoken. "I have friends on the Council too, Tretak. Lydeck will never allow it. Never."

Tretak saw Sergeant Kuk-kek approach. "If you'll excuse me, Lieutenant," she said, departing.

Kuk-kek watched her hurry off. "What did the newcomer have to say?"

Ki-ok was too absorbed in his thoughts to hear Kuk-kek.

Sergeant Kuk-kek stepped a little closer. "Sir?"

Ki-ok snapped out of his daydream with a start. "Huh? Tretak? She had nothing to say. But she is not a newcomer, Sergeant. Not a newcomer. She has been here before."

CHAPTER 20

Lydeck scurried through the stone corridors, continuously looking back to see if he had been followed. Leeg followed close behind remaining oddly quiet and compliant. The fledgling's cooperation and silence was beginning to grate Lydeck's nerves. He wondered why the youngster had gone along so easily, with only the slightest bit of protest. "I am a member of the Council after all." Lydeck snapped his head to look back at Leeg. *Did I say that out loud?* he wondered.

Leeg fixed him with fearful yet oddly confident eyes. Why was the fledgling so agreeable? He ignored the thought. He had to get to the cave before Nok or Keerka knew he was gone. The only sand in the beak was that young female.

Lydeck watched the stones move under his feet, lost in thought as they walked. Down they went; every step carrying him closer to his goal of becoming Commander of the Colony. No it wasn't just the title of Commander he wanted. Now, before he carried out this act, he had to face the truth: he wanted power. He would control the fate of the colony, and anybody who defied his absolute reign would have the Royal Emperors to deal with. And when the time came, when the colony did his bidding without question, they would rise up and shake off the shackles of Royal rule. The Rockhoppers would be the means by which freedom would come. The humans, Phocids, opposing clans; all of them would fall. The

Royal Emperors were too stupid for their own good. Why try to conquer the known world when all you could want or need was right here?

"I will need a title. What shall it be?" he asked himself quietly. "Commander? No that was a title created by the Council. And the Council will no longer exist once I have things in order. Overlord?" He laughed at the thought of it. That would never work. The masses would associate him with the Royals.

Lydeck continued to muse over his possible titles. He realized that he no longer heard the scuffling and heavy breaths of Leeg. He snapped out of his musings and looked around. Leeg was nowhere to be found. What had he done? Where could he have gone, and how long ago did he leave? "Stupid," he said. Lydeck ran back the way they had come, searching in crannies and behind rocks. The kid was nowhere. What would the Shadow Warriors do to him when they found out he lost Leeg?

Lydeck's panic turned to anger. "When I find that little sea nettle, I'll take care of it then and there." He realized that they had gone past the off shoot which led to the cave. His wings slumped. "I don't deserve any of those titles. How could I be so stupid?" Leeg was gone. He was probably halfway back to the crèche by now. He would tell his father, and they would come for him, and he would die.

He was about to head toward the cave when he heard the scratch of tiny claws. He spun this way and that and spotted the young Rockhopper standing just inside the passage. Surprised by his good fortune, Lydeck composed himself and approached the fledgling. "Ah, there you are. You gave me quite a start when I noticed you were gone. Your father would have my tail-feathers if I lost you down here."

"I'm sorry, sir," Leeg said in a near whisper.

"That's fine, young one. I've found you. I promise to give you my full attention from now on." Lydeck studied Leeg. Why hadn't he run? Lydeck's eyes narrowed in suspicion. Why indeed?

"Tell me, why did you wait *here*?"

Leeg hesitated before answering. "I don't know how to get to the cave myself…and I've been lost down here before."

Lydeck relaxed. "Very good. It was wise of you to stay here. Now come along; we may not have much time."

The two walked for several minutes more. Lydeck tried to keep his mind focused on the here and now. He was hopping across a rock when an alarm went off in his head. *I never told him where we're going.* He turned back to Leeg. His eyes narrowed, boring into Leeg's eyes through the faint light. *He knows. This is part of a plan…a trap.* Lydeck was certain now that once they reached the cave that he would find the Shadow Warriors dead and Nok, accompanied by his elite squad, waiting for him. "On second thought, I don't think the cave would be a good place to hide you. I heard there is some sort of a breach in the wall. The humans might find it, and then what would we do, just the two of us?" Lydeck watched the young penguin, trying to gauge his reaction. Leeg didn't so much as twitch at hearing they wouldn't be going to his little ambush. *He's good. And so young. He would have made a great politician.* Lydeck struggled to improvise a plan. The plan he came up with made him almost giddy at the thought of his own cleverness. He hurriedly nudged Leeg back the way they had come. This would be perfect. If only the Shadow Warriors would wait another day or two.

CHAPTER 21

Keerka paced around the corridors of the warrens, silently berating her mate for being gone so long. If he took part in the attack, she'd give him hell and then some. She paced her way to the Council chambers and searched the deserted chasm for Nok. The larger-than-life emptiness of the chamber unsettled her.

She walked to the stone dais where her mate deliberated and debated with the other members of the Council. Staring out over the multileveled natural platforms, Keerka didn't envy Nok's position as Commander. Day in and day out, he dealt with the problems of the colony, all of which were laid on his back in ever increasing heaps of disillusionment, blame, subterfuge, and distrust. Nok would come back to the roost and release only part of his troubles on her. They would discuss the best course of action and his worries would ease. Keerka was his counsel and his strength, and he knew that. He often said that she would be the better Commander, but Keerka had no desire to take that post; it was enough to be an outsider let alone be directly involved.

Lost in her thoughts and worry, Keerka hadn't noticed Packt enter the chamber. "If you're hoping for a place on the Council, my time is short," Packt said.

Keerka jumped and gave her a wry look. "I'm sure you will outlive most of us, Packt. There are rumors that you're immortal."

"Even if that were true, I wouldn't want it. What motivation would I have to live if I couldn't die?"

The crotchety old matriarch waddled her way in front of Keerka and stood solid and still. Keerka watched and waited for her to say something more. When enough time had gone by for Keerka to think the old Rockhopper had fallen asleep, she looked around, wondering what to do next. "Uh, Packt, are you still with us?"

Packt's eyes snapped open. "Us? Who else is here?"

"I think you were lost in a dream somewhere."

"Dreams, reality; one can't exist without the other." When Keerka only replied with a blank stare, Packt continued, "I'm glad you're here. I've been meaning to speak with you."

"About?"

"Your son has grown close to Kicki, correct?"

"Yes, the two are the best of friends. Why do you ask?"

Packt waddled slowly back and forth, her slow motion version of pacing. "Have you heard stories of the Oracle?"

"Of course. I think every penguin has heard of that legend."

"A legend is just a memory shared by many. I've been watching Kicki from afar. She...tell me, have you ever noticed her do anything which you might consider unusual? For example, talk about an event which has yet to take place or that doesn't pertain to the colony?"

"She...she sometimes seems to drift away and sway as she stands. But she doesn't seem to be aware that she does it. Shouldn't you be discussing this with her parents? Why me?"

"I will speak to them in good time. But you know how they are; they are rather closed off from the rest of the colony and not very keen on radical ideas. And I ask you because Kicki spends more time with Leeg and you than at her own roost."

"Are you saying what I think you're saying? That Kicki could be an Oracle? Oracles are the things of legend—they're not real."

"Don't be so sure, Keerka. I have been around a very long time. I know a lot about what a lot do not know. And I say to you that the Oracle is real—or was real."

"Was?"

Packt hesitated before answering. "I have been touched by that gift. But only slightly. I have never been able to control it or see beyond our own colony. If I had, I might have saved Nok's parents." Packt looked away.

"That wasn't your fault. No one is to blame except those humans. They're the ones who killed them."

"From that day on I knew Nok would have his beak in future events; events gone past and events yet to come." Packt averted her eyes. "But that is not why I'm here."

"If there is something you're not telling me about Nok…"

"Nothing but only the vaguest of impressions. All I know is that his part in the greater war is not yet over, and neither is yours."

Keerka turned away. No more wars, no more fighting. She wanted nothing to do with it. She just wanted to raise a family and live a normal penguin's life. "So what about this Oracle?" she asked tiredly.

"The Oracle is dead. She did not die a natural death. She was murdered."

"I'm sure that was a long time ago. Whoever it was who killed her is dead too, right?" Keerka didn't like the way this conversation was going.

"No. She died only yesterday. Killed violently."

"How could you know that? I thought you said your gift was weak?"

"I know…I had to know. The currents carried this information to me in a dream. And I know that once Lapasia's killer finds out about Kicki, he will come for her. When she is fledged, she will have to go into hiding."

"Hiding?" Keerka was appalled. "She will be safe here. The Rockhoppers of this colony will protect her to their deaths."

"And that is why she has to leave. If the colony found out about her abilities, word would spread. Before long, thousands of penguins would arrive, all to beseech her with their futures, and it would be then that he would find her."

"Leeg would be lost without her. The two are like two halves to a clam. They—"

"That is why he will have to go with her."

Keerka's eyes lost all expression. "No. After everything Nok has been through, to have his first hatched taken away might prove to be too much for him. I'm no stranger to loss. My previous mate and I lost three offspring; none survived to maturity, and then he was taken by poachers. I don't want to lose Leeg too."

"Some say the Ancients have their own reasons for taking those we love."

"To hell with the Ancients." Keerka began to walk out, but stopped. "Who is *he*? This killer."

Packt shifted her corpulent frame. "He is our doom."

Keerka ruffled her feathers. "Our doom?" she said, turning to face Packt.

"Aperion. He is of an ancient race. A race that if allowed to propagate, will destroy and subjugate all penguins as Antaean attempted to do. Their race is much more powerful than the Royal Emperors." Packt waited for Keerka to ask more, but with no questions forthcoming, she continued. "I was once on the Council of Thrace. It was there that I learned of him and his brother Saeson. Aperion will seek his queen by any means. I only hope that Lapasia, the Oracle, misled him."

"If this council knew he was a threat, why is he still alive? Why didn't they just kill him?"

"Ill-guided belief that they were doing good is the best answer I can give you. And that is all I can tell you. Kicki is who matters now, and she must be protected at all costs. She may be our hope for survival."

"This is all too much. Is this why you said Nok and I will be part of the war?"

"I can only assume. You will have to tell Commander Nok."

"Honestly, Packt, I think it would be best coming from you. He respects you more than you know."

"I have my beak full enough. Nok's enemies may be attempting to oust him as Commander. I will do what I must to prevent that from happening." Packt nuzzled her beak against Keerka's. "Take care of him. He needs you. You are the wave which carries him to shore. It is the both of you who are two halves to a clam."

Keerka watched the old matriarch waddle away with a wistful sentiment burgeoning in her heart. "Why did I never take the time to befriend her before?" She mulled over all Packt had said and thoughts carried her to Kicki. Kicki was as sweet a Rockhopper as she had ever known, and she wished the little one had a different fate. As she thought of Kicki, urgency welled up inside of her. For whatever reason, she felt she had to get to her immediately.

CHAPTER 22

Lydeck entered the Council chamber through one of its side entrances, Leeg in tow. He watched as Commander Nok entered, followed by Lieutenant Ki-ok and Colonel Kairg, who were each presenting their versions of some sort of dispute between the two. He ushered Leeg forward and stepped in close to hear the argument.

"Commander, please hear me out," Ki-ok said. "The Colonel clearly disregarded orders. Disregarded. And I am certain he did it just to steal the glory for himself. He has done it in the past, sir. He has done it in the past."

"Lieutenant, where did Colonel Kairg engage the enemy?" Nok asked.

Ki-ok hesitated. "In the surf, sir."

"Correct. What were your orders?"

"To secure the beach and ensure that no humans, *no* humans, touched foot on land."

Nok stared at Ki-ok in silence.

Ki-ok cleared his throat. "And to confront the enemy, confront him in the surf."

"Precisely, Lieutenant."

"We were set to attack, all set when we spotted Colonel Kairg's team engaging the enemy. You can ask Sergeant Kuk-kek. Ask him."

"If I may interject, Commander?" Kairg asked. Nok nodded his approval. "We were in pursuit of our prey. In fact, had it not been for

Tretak's quick thinking, the human might have eluded us. She is clever and quick-minded. I would like to see her given a proper rank…perhaps lieutenant."

Ki-ok began to bark about being slighted when Commander Nok silenced him with a stern glare. The Lieutenant slumped back. "You will tell me more about this later, Colonel. We can always use a penguin who can demonstrate ingenuity. Now, Lieutenant Ki-ok, given the circumstances, I do not see how the colonel was out of line." Ki-ok once again began to protest. Nok hissed a warning. "In fact, had I had messengers available to me, Colonel Kairg would have been informed of your assignment. But I didn't, and he is not to be blamed for my lack of foresight. I'm sorry if you feel he did this on purpose…he didn't. As far as charges of insubordination—I think we can all agree that this was just a misunderstanding, and no charges should be brought upon the lieutenant." It wasn't a suggestion.

Colonel Kairg nodded his agreement.

Lydeck, still standing afar, perked up at hearing Commander Nok's own admission of failure. Perhaps he could use this piece of information. Leeg started to walk toward his father, but Lydeck hushed him. "Your father is in an important discussion. It would be unwise for you to interrupt him."

Leeg stepped back, never taking his eyes off of Lydeck.

"I'm sure, if the situation had presented itself, you would have performed admirably, Lieutenant," Nok said.

"But, but sir," K-ok continued.

"There will be no more discussion, Lieutenant. We should be celebrating our victory, not debating over who was responsible for it. We are all responsible…all of us. This is the colony's victory, not any one Rockhopper." Nok turned away and noticed Leeg standing with Lydeck in the shadows. "Leeg, what are you doing here? Why aren't you with the crèche?"

Lydeck answered before Leeg could say a word. "My apologies, Commander. With the talk of a human invasion, I took it upon myself to see young Leeg here to safety."

Nok's eyes narrowed. "Invasion? It was one small craft. You knew that."

"Yes, sir. But with the flying machines nearby and rumors within the warrens about a possible infiltration, I thought it would be wise to protect our leader's only offspring. If something were to happen to him, I could never live with myself and I doubt you could either, sir." Lydeck waited for a response, doing his best to keep his composure under Nok's accusing glare. "Or was I overzealous in my duties?"

Nok's expression softened. "No, Lydeck. But in the future, leave the protecting to his parents. That is not a request."

Lydeck swallowed hard for show. "Yes sir. My apologies again."

Nok ignored Lydeck to call for Sergeant Trarck. Lydeck stood nearby to eavesdrop once again.

"Yes Commander?" Trarck said as he huffed through a nearby passage.

"Victory is ours at last. Gather the Council. I want them assembled when I return." Nok called to Leeg, who happily ran to his side.

Trarck looked at the two questioningly.

"We'll talk later. Call for assembly—I have an important announcement to make."

∧∧∧

Lydeck watched Nok and Trarck leave and noticed that that obnoxious Colonel Kairg was gone too. He slinked up to Lieutenant Ki-ok. "It's a shame, Lieutenant, a real shame that Commander Nok doesn't appreciate a Rockhopper of your talents. Why, I'm certain that a Rockhopper of your abilities could have easily defeated the encroachers."

Ki-ok lifted his downcast head. "It is good to know that I have at least one supporter on the Council. Very good to know."

"One? No, there are more, but Commander Nok and some others still blame you for their own failures."

Ki-ok stared at the stone beneath his feet.

"Why if I became Commander, I would have you promoted at once to

General, or perhaps War Chief."

"But you are not the commander. Not commander."

Lydeck moved closer to Ki-ok. "I could be. In fact, I will be."

"How could you? Nok's supporters hold the majority."

"I have powerful allies. Nok plans to have Trarck replace him as Commander. This will solidify Nok's legacy of nepotism, division, and failure. The unity we have worked so hard for is beginning to crumble. You've seen it; we have all seen it." Lydeck circled Ki-ok, keeping his eyes fixed on the lieutenant. "What if I told you there are plans already in motion to oust Nok as Commander?"

"How? A coup?"

"If it comes to that. But I prefer a slightly more peaceful measure. Nok's majority is really only held by a margin of one. If we were to say…convince that one member to resign from the Council, she could be replaced by someone who could be controlled and vote in our favor. I will become Commander and you will be my War Chief."

"She? Who is she? And how would we convince her? How?"

Lydeck looked around to make sure there were no ears close by. "Packt. She is the one."

Ki-ok slumped. "Packt will never resign. Never."

"That is why you must convince her. You and the squads you command."

Ki-ok swallowed nervously. "If we attempt to intimidate her, she will tell Sergeant Trarck and we would be ousted ourselves. Ousted. And she will still hold her seat."

Lydeck leaned in close to Ki-ok's ear. "Packt is old. If she were to have an accident, it would never be suspected that it was otherwise."

"Murder. What you're suggesting is murder. If we were caught or even suspected we would be tried and executed. Executed."

"That is why it must look like an accident. Old penguins stumble and fall all the time."

"I can't. I cannot. Packt has never said an ill word toward me. Never."

Lydeck stood tall and let out a long breath. "Suit yourself, Lieutenant. Continue to be marginalized until you are finally stripped of your rank. I can only do so much from my Council seat."

Ki-ok's eyes went wide. "Why? Why would they do that to me?"

"When Trarck becomes Commander, he will clean the roost of those he sees as…unnecessary. And I know that is how he views you. Or," Lydeck lifted Ki-ok's beak with his own, "you could be War Chief, and together we could bring unity and stability to the colony. You will be seen as a hero who helped shape our colony's glorious future. And the false accusations of cowardice during the war will be long forgotten." Lydeck watched with satisfaction as Ki-ok struggled with his thoughts. He did have every intention of bestowing the created title of War Chief on the lieutenant, but what Ki-ok didn't know was that the title was merely honorific, and a temporary one at that. In no way would Lydeck ever put Ki-ok in charge of any of his forces. The lieutenant was indecisive and a failure as an officer. After that, Ki-ok was a loose end to be discarded.

Lydeck began to lose his patience with Ki-ok's indecisiveness. "Or…"

Ki-ok perked up. "Or what? What or are you speaking of?"

"I could make Colonel Kairg the War Chief. I'm sure he would jump at the opportunity to have the glory to himself." If a penguin could smile, Lydeck would have right then. He had him.

Ki-ok's eyes lit up with anger. "No. No, I will not allow it." He looked around the chamber conspiratorially. "You do promise to make me War Chief? You promise?"

"You have my word." Lydeck watched Ki-ok wrestle one last time with his decision.

Ki-ok nodded. "I'll do it—I will do what you ask. But I'll do it alone."

"Excellent. This must be done immediately, before she is roused for the Council and those accursed apprentices return."

"I will convince her to step down."

"And if she doesn't agree to?"

Ki-ok looked at Lydeck but said no more and rushed away.

Lydeck let out a satisfied breath and watched the future War Chief disappear down the dark corridor. "This was almost too easy."

CHAPTER 23

Keerka strolled through the warrens with a troubled heart. Kicki, an Oracle? It was too much to believe. Keerka recalled something General Treeg had said. *'If you listen intently you might find the answer before the question is posed.'* Did he know of the Oracle? She was certain that he had. There was very little Treeg didn't know. She doubted that he knew that he would be killed at Isla Sola. Or maybe he did, maybe that was his intention; to pass his legacy on to the next generation. Whatever the reason, he was dead, and that was that. Keerka wasn't going to spend time trying to figure out how a soothsayer's mind worked. She knew what she had to do—protect Kicki at all costs until she matured enough to make the journey to wherever she was supposed to go. If Packt knew of Kicki's ability, then somebody else might know as well. Hopefully, that somebody wasn't Aperion. "Whoever or whatever Aperion is."

Keerka considered going back to speak with Packt. There was so much to know; so much that Treeg hadn't told her, and the matriarch had the answers. She stopped and deliberated while scratching her neck on a well-worn stalagmite. No, it could wait; she had to check on Leeg and Kicki, Packt would be there. Kicki was the priority, not her curiosity.

^^^

Kicki tried to see past the crowds of Rockhoppers milling about the main passage. She overheard talk of a long-awaited peace and rumors of the

Council electing a new Commander. It meant very little to Kicki. All she cared about was finding an adult who would listen to her. She stared in the direction Lydeck had taken Leeg and the world began to swirl around her. Images flashed in her mind: a strange looking penguin with yellow eyes, a shadow looming over the yellow-eyes penguin, a large black and white sea creature. She didn't understand what she saw. Her head swirled and she was vaguely aware that her body rocked and swayed. She imagined it was like swimming in the sea, though she had never been in the water.

She saw Leeg; he was much older. She saw him again, but at his present age. A Shadow Warrior stood over him; Lydeck was there. Leeg was in danger, waves crashed nearby—the cave, they were in the cave. She had to save him, but she couldn't get to him. The penguin with the yellow eyes appeared once more; a terrible and large penguin with a beak longer than any Rockhopper was tall stood behind her. The yellow-eyes appeared before her face. All she could see were the yellow irises, almost as if they were touching her. The strange penguin spoke to her. "*Kicki of the Northern Rockhoppers, the gift is now yours alone. Guard it well. He will come for you but, he will not find you.*" Kicki's vision turned to violence: Rockhoppers dying; the big penguin ripping them to pieces with his enormous beak; blood, death, calls of pain. The yellow eye appeared before her once more. "*What you see does not have to be; fate is never fate. Be strong, Kicki. Fear does not dwell within you, it can only be put upon you. Kicki...Kicki.*" The voice became familiar. She knew the voice. Her mind's eye swirled and it seemed as if she had suddenly awoke.

"Kicki."

The young Rockhopper looked up and found Keerka standing before her. Where had she come from?

"Kicki," Keerka said, warning away bustling penguins. "What are you doing out here? You should be inside, dear. You might get run over."

Kicki looked up, her eyes wide. "Keerka. It's Leeg—we have to go." She began to jabber so quickly that Keerka had a hard time understanding what she was saying.

"All right, all right. Slow down," Keerka said in a calm motherly voice. "Now what about Lydeck and Leeg?"

"He's taken Leeg. He's the other voice we heard talking to the Shadow Warrior. It's Lydeck. He's up to something bad. I know it. He's going to hurt Leeg," Kicki said, forcing herself to slow down.

Keerka tried to hide her fear. "Now, why would he want to hurt Leeg? And where did he take him?"

"I don't know," Kicki said. "But he *was* the one who we heard talking to the Shadow Warrior. He said something about protocols and that he had to take him to a safe place before the humans arrive."

Keerka stared at Kicki, her slick feathers in a ruffle. There were no protocols. "All right, sweetie. Listen to me. There are no humans coming here. Do you understand? The humans have been taken care of."

Kicki nodded. "I know."

"Can you tell me which way they went?"

Kicki pointed toward the passage Lydeck had taken Leeg. "Down. Back to the cave." Even though Keerka was trying her best not to show that she was scared, Kicki knew she really was, and that scared her even more. And the things she saw were never wrong.

Keerka stared at the passage and it seemed as if she were considering going after Lydeck alone. She guided Kicki back into the crèche. "I need you to stay here. Promise me that you'll stay inside with the crèche minder. Do not leave for any reason."

"All right, I promise," she said, her voice a frightened whisper.

"I'm going to get Commander Nok, and we'll find out where they went. Remember, stay here." Keerka told the crèche minder to make sure she stayed put. She turned and stopped to nuzzle Kicki's beak for reassurance and hurried to catch Nok before the Council arrived.

CHAPTER 24

Nok and a small group of his most trusted advisors were gathered in an alcove adjacent to the Council chamber. Leeg stood among several large rocks, trying to remain inconspicuous while his father discussed business that he had no part of. With the exception of replying to a few well-meaning adults who took the opportunity to remark on the speed of his growth, he remained quiet and sullen.

"I believe a celebration is in order. You have finally led us to complete victory. I will make a motion for a celebration," Council member Melk said enthusiastically.

"There will be time enough for celebration later. This meeting will be about finding my successor."

Melk, Cleyed, and Cosk immediately began issuing adamant protests.

"Sir," said Cosk. "Savor your victory, if only for today. I understand your fatigue. The war, the fights; but now is not the time."

"You're wrong, Cosk. Now is the perfect time. My presence on the Council has been divisive. Lydeck's supporters are once again growing. If I don't act now, the one I hope to replace me might not receive the majority vote."

"And who is your choice?" Cleyed asked.

Colonel Kairg, who had remained silent up to that point, chimed in before Nok could answer. "I hope it's not me you're considering. I'm a fighter, not a politician."

"Don't worry, Colonel. It's not you," Nok replied. Kairg tried to conceal a huff of indignity.

The others waited anxiously. Each of them were well versed in the politics of Rockhopper government, but none truly desired to shoulder the responsibilities of Colony Commander.

"My choice is Sergeant Trarck," Nok finally said, easing their fears.

Melk and Cosk looked at one another, Melk shrugged, and the two agreed with the decision. Cleyed, on the other hand, wasn't so quick to agree, "I'm sorry, sir, but I'm not sure he would be the best choice. Despite his stellar service to the colony, his youth might be used against him when it comes to the vote."

"There is nobody else I would trust more as leader of the Ministry. I have never seen him perform a selfish act in all of the time I've known him. He's stalwart and intelligent, and has shown he can handle the stress of the Council. And as you well know, he can even put them in their place when the squabbling gets out of control. If there is somebody else you have in mind, please let me know."

Cleyed seemed to mull over Nok's assessment of Trarck. "I see your point, Commander. I guess you're right. He makes most other penguins seem subpar."

Nok laughed. "I wouldn't say subpar, but I'm glad you agree. Well, that's settled; now about bringing it to a vote? If Packt votes our way, and I have no reason to think she wouldn't, then Trarck could be installed as soon as tomorrow."

"Are you sure Packt will vote for Trarck? We're not really giving anybody else a chance to throw their name into the pool," Cosk said.

"Lydeck will make a move, I'm certain. He won't like it, but I am Commander, and my word is the rule. And I'm sure Packt will see things our way. In fact I can almost guarantee it." Nok couldn't help but notice

Leeg's body tense when he heard Lydeck's name mentioned. "I suggest we prepare for the meeting now."

"What about the sergeant?" Kairg asked. "Who will replace Trarck as Sergeant of the Council of Order?"

Nok looked at the others for suggestions, but none were forthcoming. "That is still open for discussion, Colonel."

Colonel Kairg stepped to center. "If I may make a suggestion—why not Tretak? She is already up for commendation. She is intelligent, devoted, fierce, and quite cunning. She would be perfect for the position."

"Can we trust her? She has been with the colony for only a short time and I haven't had an opportunity to get to know her. Are you sure she would be a good fit?"

"Absolutely, Commander," said Kairg.

Melk stood to the side, looking as is if his beak were about to crack open. When it appeared that Nok had nothing more to say, he broke in. "I have had the pleasure to speak with Tretak on many occasions. She is an absolute delight. She is everything the Colonel says she is and much, *much* more. She is as solid as any Rockhopper I've met, she is a magnificent conversationalist—I should know; we are practically neighbors and I make it a point to engage her in the most interesting of conversations at every opportunity. Our discussions cover a variety of topics, and not just about squid or fish or the waves. For example, we talk about what makes the waves roll across the sea and why light leaks through the blanket of night. And let me tell you, she is quite well versed in the stories of the Ancients. Her mellifluous voice is at once calming and endearing, resting upon the bedrock of strength and confidence. She shows no signs of weakness, nor does she display fealty to any uncertain past times, I assure you that. I wholeheartedly endorse her for sergeant and would a thousand times over…if I could." Melk looked around the room and realized the others were staring at him in silence. "I mean, it's just that she is…qualified. Very qualified."

Nok spoke first to break the silence. "It sounds like that's settled. I trust the Colonel's word and after Melk's exuberant, if not...*amorous* endorsement, I believe she will fit in quite nicely."

"Agreed," the others said in unison.

Nok let out a satisfied breath. "Great. Now if you'll excuse me, I need to bring Leeg back to the crèche before Keerka—"

"Nok, Lydeck has taken Leeg," Keerka said, bursting into the chamber.

"Keerka. Keerka," he said with more insistence. "He's fine. He's right here."

Keerka spotted Leeg and rushed to him. "Are you all right? Did he hurt you?"

"No mama, I'm all right," Leeg said, his voice sounding small amongst the chattering adults.

"Wait, hold on," Kairg said, walking to Nok. "Why would Lydeck have your son?"

"That's what I intend to find out," Nok said. "He said he was acting out of concern—that he feared the humans would infiltrate the warrens—so he brought him to safety. But his lie was weak."

"Nok," Keerka interrupted. "There's more to it. I spoke with Kicki, and she said she recognized the voice they heard speaking to the Shadow Warrior."

"Shadow Warrior?" Kairg blurted. Nok raised a flipper.

Keerka looked at her son. "Is Kicki telling the truth?"

Leeg looked at the adults, who were eyeing him with concern. "Yes. It was Lydeck."

Kairg looked at Nok. "Shadow Warriors, Commander?"

"Yes. The fledglings were playing away from the crèche when Leeg and Kicki got separated. They found the cave at the bottom of the warrens and heard voices. They said they saw a Shadow Warrior and a Rockhopper. We dismissed it as over active imaginations and Tearsk telling them scary stories."

"Why wasn't I notified?" Kairg demanded. "My squads would make short work of those accursed Royals."

Nok looked to Keerka; he knew that secret operations wouldn't look good, especially among his most trusted allies. "I conducted a quiet investigation. Before you protest, you know if word got out about Royals being here, it would cause a general panic. And I'm sure my opponents would have jumped on it to further undermine my authority. In the end, the investigation team found no evidence of any Shadow Warriors. No guano, no pinfeathers, nothing. There was nothing to go on...until now."

Cosk stepped in. "We should have Lydeck brought up on charges. He is a traitor and should be dealt with accordingly."

"I appreciate your enthusiasm, Cosk. But we need more evidence. I seriously doubt that the Tribunal will execute a member of the Council of Order based solely on the word of two fledglings. That is one of the reasons behind the apprenticeship. Lydeck was right, I initiated it to watch him. But given what we know now, it was well-founded."

"I agree with Cosk," Kairg said. "I say we bypass the Tribunal altogether. We find him and execute him on the spot."

"And what happens to the rule of law?" Nok asked. "No. As much as I'd like to, and I'm certain Keerka would as well, we have to maintain order or else we'll find ourselves the disbanded colony of squabbling Rockhoppers we were before Treeg reestablished the Ministry."

"Should we postpone the assembly?" asked Melk.

Nok shook his head. "No. We have to carry on as if we don't suspect anything. Right now, Lydeck doesn't think we know anything, and that works to our advantage. At the very least we will know his whereabouts."

"But why would he take Leeg?" Cosk asked again. "Sure, he views you as a political adversary; but kidnapping?"

"My only guess he is doing things to distract me from my duties so he can show the Council my inability to focus on the job. If he is in collusion with Royals, then it could be something else, something worse."

He looked at Keerka to gauge her reaction, but she remained unusually quiet. Nok guessed it was the stress of finding Leeg gone. "Colonel, assign Tretak to guard the crèche. That will be her first assignment as Sergeant of the Council. Tell her nobody takes any fledglings except for the parents. Absolutely nobody. No exceptions."

Kairg nodded and began to leave, but stopped. "Should she know why we are doing this?"

"No. Not yet. The fewer penguins who know, the better. I will fill her in later."

The others followed Kairg from the room leaving only Nok, Keerka and Leeg. "I had a long conversation with Packt. Kicki needs to be protected as well," Keerka said.

"The whole crèche should. But why Kicki?" Nok guided Keerka away from Leeg.

Keerka studied her mate for moment. "The fewer who know the better. I will tell you soon."

"You can't tell me? We're pair bonded for life, and there is also that little fact that I'm the Commander."

Keerka made a slight head movement toward Leeg. "I'm taking Leeg back to the crèche."

With Keerka gone, Nok was left to his thoughts. He paced around the alcove, deliberating his next move and wondering how it had gotten so bad. He felt that old familiar rage welling up inside of him, the rage he had felt when he killed his first human; the rage that had carried him through the war. "Kairg's right. I should just kill him now."

"Kill who?" a voice came from the wide entryway.

Nok spun around. "Tretak. I'm sorry, I didn't see you come in. I was just crashing the wave against the rock, so to speak."

"I apologize, Commander. I'm looking for Colonel Kairg, and was told he would be here."

"He was. Actually he's looking for you. I have given you an assignment, but I'll let the Colonel fill you in. He should be headed toward your roost."

Tretak stared at Nok for moment. "Then I will take my leave." She raised her beak in a salute and left.

"No, wait. Stay for a moment; we need to talk."

Tretak hesitantly walked in the alcove.

"I heard you used to live here. Is that true? And if so, why did you leave?"

Tretak took a long breath. "It is true, I did live here before. I've spent most of the past few seasons at sea…alone. I left after my mate was killed by the humans before the war. We had eggs, but they were lost. With nothing for me here, I just left."

"So why come back? Are you hoping to start over?"

Tretak hesitated before answering. Her eyes showing Nok that she was trying decide what to say. "I have some unfinished business to take care of."

CHAPTER 25

Kicki stood as close to the entry as she possibly could without attracting attention, hoping to catch a glimpse of Leeg's parents as they passed by to rescue her friend. They were taking far too long, and the memory of her visions increased her anxiety. She stepped back inside and began pacing once again. She tried to call on her foresight to check on his safety, but she couldn't call it at will. But she couldn't just stay in the crèche while her best friend was in danger. "I can't just stay here, Leeg would do the same for me," she said to herself. He always protected her; now it was her turn.

She looked at the crèche minder, who was keeping her old but watchful eye on her. She couldn't just run out. As it stood, she didn't feel good about breaking her promise to Keerka, but a good scolding was the least of her worries. She scanned the room, trying to formulate a plan to escape. Her eyes fell on a feisty young male and she knew she had found her target. "Papo, come here."

Papo swiveled his head, found who had called him, and promptly ignored her.

Kicki clenched her beak. Why did he have to be so difficult? She tried again. "Pap-po, come here." Papo looked at her again and sauntered in her general direction. If he moved any slower, he'd be mistaken for a rock.

He stood over Kicki, doing his best to intimidate her. Kicki wasn't impressed.

"What do you want? Where'd your boyfriend go?" the irascible youth asked.

"He went back to his nest," she said, ignoring his taunts. "Hey, do you know what I heard?"

"How am I supposed to know what you heard? And why would I care?" He started to walk away.

Kicki was in danger of losing her distraction. "Well if you don't want to know what Cykel has been saying about you, then go ahead and leave." Papo stopped and Kicki let out a sigh of relief. The two adolescents were gaining fame for their frequent scraps.

"What did he say?" Papo demanded, scrunching his eyes in anger.

"If you're not going to ask nicely, then never mind."

"Tell me before I peck it out of you," he snapped.

"He said if you had any intelligence in that empty shell of a head of yours, you'd realize that your breath smells like guano and that's why nobody likes you." Kicki took a step back in case he decided to take his anger out on her.

"He said that?" He turned and spotted Cykel in the crowd who, to Kicki's good fortune, happened to be laughing when their eyes met.

Within seconds, the two youths were yelling at one another, and two seconds after that they were in an all-out brawl. The crèche minder ran to break up the fight, giving Kicki her break. She snorted. "Boys...sometimes it's just too easy." She slipped out of the crèche chamber and made a dash for the passage.

CHAPTER 26

Keerka walked with Leeg along the passageways. While she was relieved that Leeg was safe, she couldn't help but to be a little upset that he had left the crèche in the first place. She looked down at her son. "Tell me, son. Why did you leave with Lydeck? You're not in trouble, I promise you that. I just need to know what you were thinking."

Leeg hesitated until Keerka reassured him with a caress from her beak. "I hoped Kicki would tell you so that everybody would believe us about what we saw. I knew it was Lydeck as soon as he spoke to us."

"Us? You mean he talked to Kicki too?"

"Yes. She tried to come with us, but I told her to stay. She knew what she had to do."

Keerka became more concerned. If Lydeck was up to something, which she had no doubt he was, then that meant that Kicki might be in danger too. "Where did he take you?"

"I already told Father."

"But you haven't told me," Keerka said as she picked up her pace. She felt an urgency to get to Kicki.

"I think he was taking me to the cave. I'm pretty sure; it's hard to tell in the dark." Leeg struggled to keep up with his mother. "But we turned around and he took me the back way to the Council room."

Keerka shuddered. Leeg might have been killed. Keerka stopped. The pieces were coming together. "A distraction," she said softly. It hit her like a wave pounding against a rock. Lydeck intended to kill Leeg. He must have been. Nok would be devastated and unable to lead and Lydeck would take the opportunity to usurp him. *To hell with law*, Keerka thought. *I'll kill Lydeck myself.* But first she had to get Leeg to the crèche. He would be safe under the watchful eye of the new crèche minder. And Tretak would be there to ensure he'd be safe.

When they arrived she heard the angry squawking of young Rockhoppers and the equally angry call of Eeco. She burst into the room to find Eeco attempting to break up a fight. Keerka guided Leeg to the farthest wall and walked into the midst of the fight. "That is enough." Her voice echoed off of the stone walls and the entire cavern became instantly silent.

Every Rockhopper in the room stared wide-eyed at Keerka. "What is the meaning of this?" The ferocity of her demand made even the crèche-minder afraid to speak. Keerka looked at her, waiting for an answer.

"Um, the boys got into a squabble and I was attempting to break it up."

Keerka's gaze fell on the two young Rockhoppers. The combatants huddled together in fear. "If you so much as look at one another cross-eyed again, I will have your tail feathers and I'll follow you home I will take your parent's as well. Do you un-der-stand?" The two nodded, unable to find the courage to speak.

Keerka turned to Eeco, whose eyes were as wide as clam shells. She desperately wanted to reprimand the old Rockhopper, but to do so in the crèche would undermine her authority. Instead she took her aside and spoke to her quietly. "You need to be more assertive. You have a soft spot for the young ones, I know. But they will run wild if you aren't stern with them."

"I apologize. I will do my best. It's not an easy task."

"Things have changed, Eeco. Hopefully we can all go back to the way things were very soon. The crèche won't be as necessary when that happens."

Leeg came to Keerka's side, trying to get her attention. "I'm talking, Leeg. Give me a moment."

"But mother, Kicki is gone."

Keerka whirled around to her son. "Gone?"

Leeg swallowed hard. "Yes. She's not here."

Ice ran up Keerka's spine. She glared at Eeco, then searched the room herself. "Has anybody seen Kicki?" The fledglings looked about, then almost uniformly, shook their heads. "Leeg, you stay here. No matter what, do not leave with anybody except your father or me."

"I won't. I'll wait for you here. Find her."

The fear in Leeg's eyes made Keerka's heart ache. This was all too much. She nuzzled his beak and left. Once outside of the crèche she nearly ran into Colonel Kairg and Tretak.

"What's the hurry?" Kairg asked lightheartedly. The look in Keerka's eyes told him all he needed to know. "I'll muster a search squad. Tretak, make sure no fledglings leave."

"I will, sir. What's going on? Why the alarm?"

"I'll debrief you later. Just be diligent." He looked to Keerka, who was already leaving. "Is it Leeg? Which way are you going?"

"I'm headed to the lower passages. It's not Leeg. I swear, if Lydeck is behind this one as well, there won't be anything left of him to stand trial."

"I'm for doing that even if he isn't behind this." After Keerka rushed off, he turned to Tretak. "You're up for more than a commendation. I promise you, you're going to like what we have in store for you."

Tretak began to speak, but Kairg didn't wait around for a reply. After making sure Kairg and Keerka were out of sight, Tretak scanned the nearly empty corridor and slipped away.

CHAPTER 27

Ki-ok made his way up the dark passageway which led to Packt's chamber. Fortunately for him, Packt's self-imposed segregation from the rest of the colony made the chances of him being seen slim. He steeled his nerves and pressed forward. This was the only way. He had to prove that he wasn't a coward, and when he became War Chief, he would exile that obnoxious Colonel Kairg. He thought about that day, reveled in it. He imagined himself standing on a cliff edge watching Kairg swim away in disgrace.

And then there was Commander Nok. What had he ever actually done to deserve his post? Sure he killed a man, but many Rockhoppers had killed many men. He led the attack on the attack on the poacher's ship, but if it weren't for the Gentoo, the attack would have failed. And nobody could verify that he had actually been there to help kill Supreme Commander Liutites, they just accepted his and Keerka's word. His position was based solely on his relationship with General Treeg. In fact it was Nok's attempt to rescue Keerka that had gotten General Treeg killed. All of his exploits during the war had led to the deaths of other Rockhoppers. No wonder Lydeck wanted him out.

Ki-ok's internal diatribe ended when he reached the top of the corridor. Light streamed in from a small aperture in the cliff wall, its focused beam reflected off of gray stone, only to be swallowed up by the darkness in the path he had taken. His crest fluttered in the wind. The wind bayed like a whale's song rising from the deep as it flowed through the breach. He took a deep breath and closed his eyes; it was time to do what had to be done. "I can do this. I can." He stepped into Packt's chamber and was met with a hard slap that sent him to the ground.

"Did you come up with this brilliant plan all on your own, or did Lydeck put you up to it?" Packt said standing over the prone Rockhopper.

Ki-ok tried to shake the cobwebs from his head. Packt may have been old, fat and arthritic, but she still packed a wallop. "Plan? What plan?" Ki-ok said as he got to his feet. Another strike sent him flailing against the stone wall.

"Do not lie to me. What did he promise you in exchange for my murder? Power? A mate who would pretend to tolerate you? Glory?"

Ki-ok struggled to stand. His legs felt like two squid swimming in opposite directions. How could Packt know? There was no way she could. Somebody must have overheard. "What do you mean? What? I was merely coming to inform you that the Council meeting is about to begin. I came just to tell you." The next strike lifted him in the air and he crumbled to the ground. He rolled to his back, his eyes meeting Packt's, her corpulent frame looming over him like a storm ready to unleash its fury. Ki-ok's mind scrambled to make sense of what was happening. Packt couldn't be a mortal penguin. How else could something so slow and old strike with such ferocity? She must be one of the Ancients, alive; living here, not in some antediluvian story.

"Lies, Ki-ok. I don't need to be informed about meetings. Tell me what Lydeck is planning. Tell me now while you still have breath and I will help you," said Packt, her voice sounding less like a storm and more like a mere gale. "I know you have come to kill me. Do you think I have lived so long out of blind luck and stupidity? How does Lydeck plan to seize power? Even if you could have killed me, he wouldn't be able to wrest authority from the Council."

She knows my thoughts. How could she…how? His mind cleared enough to realize the answer: she couldn't. She was no Ancient; she merely had strong instincts, or perhaps her age made her paranoid and she made a lucky guess. If she did have insight, she would already know the answer to what she asked. Ki-ok stood and faced her. "I have not—" The next thing he knew, his back was making a painful impact on the ground.

"Lies!" Packt beat the lieutenant down one more time for good measure. "You had your chance, Ki-ok. Now *you* will have to be dealt with."

Ki-ok scrambled to get away. Sure, she was old and slow, but he was no match for her strength. The light from the breach guided his way to escape. He tried to scoot toward the light on his stomach when a great weight landed on his back. He struggled to breathe, but his lungs were pressed between the ground and whatever rock Packt had managed to heave onto his back. He felt a beak drive into the back of his skull and he was sure that he would soon die. The weight was removed, and Ki-ok realized that the rock was Packt. Odd thoughts filled his head while he struggled for consciousness. Her body was hard and unyielding, not soft and forgiving like one might expect from a bigger Rockhopper. His senses came back when his lungs were once again greeted with oxygen.

Ki-ok tried to stand, but saw Packt getting ready to strike again. "All right, all right," he said, bracing for an impact which didn't come. He opened his eyes to find Packt huffing and staring at him.

"Well?" she said, her impatience showing through a veil of forced calm.

"It's Lydeck; it is Lydeck who is behind this. He plans to oust Commander Nok, whether by vote or coup. It was decided to rid the Council of one vote, just the one, rather than risk multiple deaths. I am sorry." Ki-ok realized he was justifying murder, and he was certain he would die soon; either by Packt, execution by the Tribunal, or by Lydeck and whoever his allies were. There was nothing left to lose. He would tell all now, but he wouldn't let them kill him. He slowly began to back toward the breach. He could feel the intensity of the wind grow as he moved closer. He would step outside and cast himself to the rocks far below. He had failed again. All of them were right, he was a failure.

"How would he manage a coup?" Packt said, matching his steps.

"He didn't say. He only told me that he had powerful allies. I presume that is how. He may have planned to use those under my command. I cannot tell you more, because I don't know more." He took a few more steps toward his freedom.

"And what were you to get out of this?" Packt matched his steps again.

"He said he would make me War Chief; that we would usher in peace, stability and unity together. That he would share that glory with me. If it wasn't me then he would make Kairg War Chief." Ki-ok knew that there would be no glory for him now, that he would always be remembered as an indecisive coward, if he was remembered at all. They would mock him and his speaking difficulties in death, as they did in life.

"Ki-ok, you poor simple-minded fool. There is no position of War Chief. You know that. If Lydeck did gain power, he would have you killed soon after to make certain nobody would know his dirty secrets."

Ki-ok's mind drifted away as Packt spoke. He was at the breach now. It would be over soon. Before he stepped out, he realized something, that he hadn't repeated his words. He felt no nervousness whatsoever. No one but him would ever know his small victory. Packt continued to prattle on about fate and law; he thought he heard something about being exiled instead of death as a punishment. Who was she to decide his fate? He would take matters into his own beak. No longer would anybody make decisions for him. He was capable and confident. Ki-ok stepped out, the wind buffeting his body as he surveyed his surroundings. Strangely enough, he could hear Packt speaking again. He hopped to the next outcropping and stared over the precipice. Death no longer held sway over him. He had no fear.

"Get back here. You will not escape your trial. I may be old, but I can still handle a penguin such as you," Packt said as she edged her way down to the outcropping.

"Old," Ki-ok said to himself. She was old; in fact she was too old to be of use to anyone. He wasn't going to be pushed around any longer. He faced Packt and looked her directly in the eye. "Old penguins have accidents all of the time." He leapt and kicked Packt in the midsection with all of his strength. The old matriarch stumbled backward and fell over the edge. Ki-ok watched her fall. She made no noise, no screams of protest; no curses were issued at him, just silence.

Ki-ok watched her hit the jagged rocks below. The Petrels were in the air already, as if they had been expecting a feast. He looked at Packt a final time and went back in to inspect her quarters, which would now be his. He considered Packt's words and replied to no one, "If Lydeck intends to kill me, I might have to kill him before he gets the chance."

CHAPTER 28

Kicki felt along the stones with her feet. The darkness seemed like a living thing which fed on a creature's vision. She forced herself to stay calm; the dark was no more alive than the stones were. A small rock clacked against another somewhere ahead of her. She listened until it finally came to rest. "Rocks aren't alive either," she whispered.

She thought of Leeg, and her fear and frustration began to well into anger. She berated herself for being stupid enough to get lost. How would she be any help to Leeg bouncing off of rocks she couldn't see? She thought about the last time she had gotten lost down there. Leeg had said to stay where they were until somebody found them.

"Leeg, Leeg, Leeg," she said as she sat, being sure to keep her voice a whisper. "I hope you're all right. I'm sorry I'm not there to help you. I really cracked the egg on this one." She rose, fidgeting. Lights began to dance and flash around her. At first she thought they were strange insects; then she realized the lights weren't flying around her head, they were *in* her head. The Seeing, as she'd come to call it, was coming. *Good*, she thought. *Maybe I can find my way back now.* However, this time the Seeing felt different, it was as if she had brought it on. She felt as if she were tugging on a wave with her beak and in an instant the flashes turned to images.

First Kicki saw Leeg. He was safe and at the crèche. Her relief was short-lived as Leeg's form melted into Keerka's. Keerka left the crèche to look for her. She was down in the cave. Kicki shuddered. Keerka was alone but not. The Shadow Warriors were there. They had her cornered; they struck relentlessly. Keerka tried to fight back, but they were too strong. The Shadows didn't stop until Keerka lay in pieces on the rocks.

Kicki tried to pull out of the Seeing; but she couldn't, it had her. She was caught in the current and had to wait for the tide to change. Next she saw Leeg again; Lydeck had him before the Shadow Warriors. Leeg was screaming. He could see what remained of his mother and fell to the ground. A Shadow Warrior took him in his beak and dashed him against the rocks. Kicki tried to scream, but her voice wouldn't come. Another wave crashed over her and brought with it more horror; Rockhopper fighting Rockhopper, Shadow Warriors striding confidently through the mayhem. Commander Nok appeared; he killed a Shadow and then went after Lydeck, who tried to run. Nok had him, but the Shadow Warriors were there; they attacked from behind, he never saw that he was about to die. Her parents were next. Lydeck and the Shadow Warriors were questioning them. Kicki understood that they were looking for her. There was another Rockhopper, someone she didn't know. Soon, her parents suffered the same fate as Leeg's. All she saw was death. Everywhere, Rockhoppers killed Rockhoppers.

The tide began to change, but the Seeing remained. This time, she saw Leeg. He was old and confidant; fierce, but loving. Tiny waves lapped at his feet, the wind teasing his crest. How could he be old if he was dead? She saw Nok and Keerka. They were someplace far away. She didn't know how she knew, only that she knew. They were among thousands of penguins; more penguins than Kicki thought existed; penguins of every size, shape, and, in some cases, color. The Seeing faded.

Kicki was aware of herself once again but she did not yet have control. But the calm was only the drawback of the sea before a tsunami. The Seeing returned, carrying with it the monstrous form of a dark penguin; its long, lethal beak preceded a frame so large it could fill the entries to any passages within the warren. The fearsome penguin looked at her with eyes blacker and colder than the deepest sea. The head grew larger. The massive beak yawned, showing deadly serrations threatening to tear flesh and crush bone. It came at her. Kicki screamed and the Seeing left her.

CHAPTER 29

Keerka heard Kicki's scream and her heart began to race. She ran toward the voice before the echo died. She deftly climbed and hopped over obstacles seen and unseen, moving through the passages on instinct alone. Thoughts of what Packt had said ran through her mind. But fortunes and war could wait. All that mattered was finding that young Rockhopper and making sure she was safe.

She entered a broken passageway where she was sure she had heard Kicki's scream. Rock lay in heaps on either side of the tunnel, and what little light had existed was extinguished as she squeezed between the rocks to enter. She hesitated. A warning chill coursed through her insulated body. Kicki was down there, she knew it, and she had to go as well. She couldn't run, and she couldn't trust instinct in the unfamiliar abyss. Keerka strained her ears, hoping to hear even the slightest sound of Kicki. It was a rare occasion that a penguin became cold, and yet her chills failed to subside even as her temper began to flare and her patience ebb. Each cautious step took a painful eternity as she willed her feet not to rush her toward the unknown.

When she felt she had gone far enough, Keerka couldn't resist calling out to Kicki. Her braying call echoed and died as suddenly as Kicki's had. She let out a breath of relief, knowing it was the odd acoustics of the narrow cavern which extinguished Kicki's call. She edged forward, carefully feeling each step. Her mind filled the gap her lack of sight had left and her imagination began to play with her. The moaning wind, coming from deep in the warrens, sounded like the dead warning her that she would join them if she didn't turn around. "No wonder Tearsk told them stories about this place. What better way to torment a young—"

Kicki's tiny voice whispered from somewhere in the dark. "Sshh, be quiet, miss Keerka."

Keerka's heart leapt with joy. "Kicki, are you all right?"

"Be quiet," Kicki answered, her voice stern and demanding.

Keerka picked up on the fledgling's fear and quieted. Kicki would never speak that way to an adult and that put fear in Keerka's heart as well. She felt her way to Kicki's side and huddled against her. "Let's go," Keerka said in her softest voice. She could feel Kicki shake her head no.

"It's close. It heard you call for me," she said in a voice so small that Keerka had trouble discerning it from the breeze.

Keerka was about to pull the girl along when she heard something in the dark, a tiny click of a tumbling pebble. Her body went rigid and she strained to hear more. The click of the pebble transformed into the tick of claws against rock, accompanied by a hiss of coarse tail-feathers whisking along the ground. Keerka put her flipper in front of Kicki. Her mind raced to formulate an escape. Whatever was down here was big and definitely not a Rockhopper. Keerka pressed her beak against Kicki's ear. "We have to go, now. You head toward where you heard me call. I will be right behind you."

"The echoes, Miss Keerka. I don't know where you were; the echoes confused me."

Before Keerka could reply, a voice seeped through the darkness. "Where to go, little Rockhoppers? Where to go? Stay where you are or try to hop away? Either way you'll be dead."

"Go back the way you came, Kicki. Go, now. I'll hold this thing off." She turned toward the Shadow Warrior. "I've dealt with your kind before. It didn't end so well for them the last time we met."

Heavy clawed feet scraped along the stone not far away. "Yes, I remember. It was I who pursued you and killed your companions. I recognized your call the moment you spoke. You will not escape a second time."

Once she was certain Kicki had done as asked, Keerka decided to taunt the Shadow. "You're the one who lived? I'd guessed that you had all died. Why else wouldn't you have come to shore to help your friend? You might have actually caught me if you hadn't been such a coward. This will make a second time that I escaped you." Keerka turned and ran. She tried to remember every rock she had stumbled over on her way down. She hopped and leapt until the black was interrupted by a slight grayness. Not much further. She hoped that Kicki was already there.

She remembered how deftly the Shadow Warriors had moved on land. They were powerful swimmers, but they could run down a tired Rockhopper if they wanted, and they very nearly had. She made a mental note to hunt down and kill every last one of them if she survived this. Keerka scrambled over a tall, smooth rock, taking advantage of the vantage point to spot her pursuer. It was closer than she had expected, just two meters behind. She spat a Rockhopper curse at the Shadow and leapt off.

The narrow entryway was just ahead. She was sure that the Shadow would be too big to fit through. After she escaped, she was going to have Nok muster the forces and come down here and kill this monster. The slap of naked feet nearby relit her urgency.

With only a few hops between her and escape, the world twisted around her and the faint gray light turned to bright white and then to black. Keerka felt a burst of pain in her head. She was aware of nothing else but her head as it hummed and pulsated in the darkness. The light returned as if to mock her as it danced in strobes before her eyes. She winced; something hard was behind her back. Rock. Why was there a rock? Her head hurt; the skin beneath her feathery crest was stinging hot. She couldn't puzzle out why she was on the ground. *Kicki.* Her mind caught up with her body. She had to get to Kicki. A slap to the other side of her head sent Keerka sprawling back to the ground. *That's right. That shadow thing.* She wasn't sure if she said it or thought it, she only knew that she couldn't fight the darkness filling her head. And then she knew it was over.

CHAPTER 30

Kicki stopped running. She never knew she could run so far so fast. When Keerka told her to go, she didn't hesitate. She was close to the central warren. Light flickered in the distance from the last of the lanterns pilfered by scavenging Rockhoppers. She could almost hear the constant chatter of the colony. Why had she stopped? She wasn't tired yet. She started forward, but stopped again. She tried to pretend she didn't know why she quit running. She could pretend no more. It was Keerka. The Shadow Warrior had her.

Kicki looked up the slope toward the warren and almost ran for safety. She closed her eyes and willed the Seeing to come to her. She imagined she was on the coast listening to the steady crashing of waves. The waves grew louder and the world grew smaller. She could see faraway places; lands of sand, of rock, of enormous bushes which touched the sky. She saw the world of man. She let her mind fall to a place of ice and snow. There was turmoil there. She wanted to see more, but she couldn't tarry any longer. She had to find Keerka, to see if she was still alive.

Wave after wave of individual Rockhoppers flew past her. She saw Nok and Lydeck. She followed them and found Leeg. She found Packt and knew she had gone to the Great Sea. She followed Ki-ok from Packt's chamber and found the path to the lower warren. She passed a void, which she knew was herself; and then the path to the darkness. At last she found Keerka.

She was alive, but unconscious. She tried to touch Keerka, to let her know help would come, but could not make contact. It was as if she were a spirit, alive but unable to live. The Seeing led Kicki to the Shadow Warrior and the near future. Keerka would be killed soon. And then she saw the only path to save Keerka.

Kicki felt as if she had been dropped to the ground when the Seeing left her. She didn't run; she simply walked toward her destination. Of all the undercurrents that had been shown to her, this was the only way. Kicki stepped through the opening and stood silent and still. And when the time came, she spoke. "If you continue along this path your death will be violent and without mercy. You will suffer, and you will suffer badly, and in the end you will die."

The Shadow Warrior swung his head toward the small Rockhopper. "You should have stayed gone, young one. Now I have two to kill."

The Seeing had shown her where every stone in the dark lay hidden. She closed her eyes and trusted her memory. She leapt from rock to rock as if it were the brightest day, being careful to stay out of the Shadow's reach.

The Shadow was visibly unnerved by the fledgling. His eyes were built to see in the dark, but a Rockhopper was just a Rockhopper. "I was going to take this one to the cave to kill her, but I see that will be a problem. Best to kill you both here."

Kicki hadn't been shown that option. Her mind raced until she realized if she hadn't seen it, then it wasn't a possibility. She forced calm upon herself once more and sought what she had seen. "Do what you must. Though, I am sure Mearna wouldn't appreciate you killing us before Lydeck takes control of the Council." Kicki had no idea who Mearna was, only that she was very powerful and, thankfully, very far away.

"What?" the Shadow snapped. "How could you know about Mearna?" He stepped toward Kicki, who made a quick retreat. "Lydeck told you. No…you overheard him. That is the only way you could know. Now, that is another one to be rid of. But first, you."

Kicki didn't try to correct him as she jumped back safely out of reach. This was not going as she had seen. Her young mind struggled to find a way to turn the tide. Despite being able to see possibilities, she didn't have the life experience to know how to outsmart a determined killer. Her head ached from trying to remember some small detail to make the Royal rethink his plans. Then it came to her. "A Council member has been killed. Lydeck had her murdered." She didn't know if that was true, but given what she had learned today it probably wasn't far from the truth. "He will have control of the Council today. If you kill us now, all of your plans will go to waste."

The Shadow Warrior stopped and Kicki tried to hide her relief. He seemed to be mulling over what she had said. He looked back at Keerka, then fixed his eyes on Kicki. "Then I will call to my brothers and we will discard your bodies in the sea, and no one will know."

Kicki tried to spit out a Rockhopper curse, but none came to her. She hopped off of her perch just as the Shadow took a swipe at her with its powerful flipper. She was down and up on another tall rock before the Shadow Warrior could recover from the missed attack. The Seeing came back in a glimpse and Kicki knew how it would end. It wasn't as it was supposed to be, but she was quickly learning that the future was rarely set. She looked toward Keerka and caught sight of her yellow head feathers moving in the feeble breeze. She hoped this wouldn't be the last time she saw her.

The Shadow Warrior struck Kicki hard enough to send her flying several feet up the passage. She gasped for breath. *That hurt. That really hurt.* She fought to take ahold of her thoughts, but all she could think about was the pain. She struggled to stand, but couldn't get her plump, fuzzy gray body to cooperate. She didn't have to see to know the Shadow Warrior was coming for her. His claws clicked on the stone, the sound of approaching doom. Fear welled up inside her and threatened to paralyze her.

In her trembling state she remembered what the penguin with the yellow eyes had said. "Fear can only be put upon on me. And I do not accept it."

The Shadow Warrior loomed over her; she could feel the breeze blocked by his large frame. It used the dark as protection, black hiding against black. Kicki kicked away before the warrior could strike. She raced toward the opening and freedom. The Shadow was inches behind her. She could almost feel the vibration of its heavy feet slapping against stone, but along with them, she heard a second pair of naked feet.

The opening was before her and she jumped as far as she had ever jumped toward the exit. The Shadow Warrior lunged, just nicking her foot before he tumbled to the ground. Kicki bounced off the stone wall and landed not a foot away from the warrior. She knew she wouldn't be able to stand before the Shadow Warrior got to his feet.

The Shadow Warrior struggled to roll to his stomach to get the leverage to stand. It had unwittingly given Kicki time to get away, but she lacked the strength to stand. She stayed still and waited. Between the Shadow Warrior's grunts of frustration as it tried to roll over, she heard the second set of footfalls. In the pallid light, she saw Keerka stumble toward the Shadow Warrior. She hopped on his chest, adding her weight to prevent him from moving. She swayed as she stood over him. In the next instant, she buried her beak in the Shadow Warrior's throat, tugging and ripping through sinewy strands of flesh until she tore his windpipe in half. She staggered off the Shadow Warrior and watched as he gurgled and twitched, making certain he would die.

Kicki stared wide-eyed at Keerka. The casual way she had killed the Shadow surprised her. She didn't know what to say when Keerka approached with blood dripping from her beak.

"You were supposed to stay in the crèche," Keerka said.

Kicki struggled to find words. "I'm sorry, Miss Keerka. I thought... and Leeg was gone. And the Seeing showed me... I'm sorry."

"It's all right. You're safe now, and so is Leeg. And that's all that matters. Now, little one, let's get out of here. We have a lot to talk about, but it'll keep 'til later." Keerka put her flipper against Kicki, guiding her, but half leaning on her as they began their walk back.

CHAPTER 31

"Commander Nok, we have another problem," Colonel Kairg said as he approached a group of Council members.

Nok lowered his head. "What now?" he said, walking away from the others.

"Another fledgling has gone missing. It's your son's friend this time. Keerka went in search of her."

Nok let out an exasperated breath. "This never ends. Send out a search party to assist her. I need you back here as soon as you can be, Colonel." With Kairg gone, Nok rejoined the Council members.

"Where is Packt? The most important Council meeting, since, well, the last meeting, and she's probably nodded off in some corner of the warren." Cosk paced nervously around the chamber. He, like the other Council members, felt nervous and antsy.

"Just stay calm. Your energy is making the rest of the Council edgy." Nok stood near the passage leading to Packt's chamber. Trarck had been gone too long for Packt to have simply fallen asleep. He studied the attending members of the Council, paying particular attention to Lydeck who seemed to be in an intense discussion with Trasik-lon. The conversation ended abruptly when Trasik-lon turned his back on Lydeck and returned to his Council perch. Nok met his eyes from across the chamber. Trasik-lon quickly broke eye contact and busied himself with preening.

"Admittedly, Packt does have a propensity to take slumber at the most unpropitious of times," Melk said, pulling Nok's attention away from Trasik-lon. "But putting her inopportune proclivities aside, which are much earned, I might add, given her progressed age, I am becoming apprehensive over her wellbeing, to such an extent that I have come to the conclusion that an extensive search of our surroundings would not be unwarranted."

Nok looked at Melk. "Duly noted." He paced around the dais, considering his options. Melk did have a point. If Trarck didn't return soon, they would have to abandon the meeting for the day until they found them. Dread ate at the pit of his stomach. "Cosk, start the benediction. We're going to have to hold the meeting without Packt. We'll consider her votes as abstained."

Cosk nodded and headed to the center of the chamber while Nok braced for a protest from Lydeck. The fact that there were no protest forthcoming made Nok feel more unsettled. It wasn't like Lydeck to not object to the even the slightest breach in etiquette of the Council meetings. He studied Lydeck once more; his smug confidence was palpable from where Nok stood. No there was something different about him today. He thought of Leeg and worry began to settle on him. He decided that now wasn't the time for the election. Nok started to call for Cosk, but his eyes caught Trarck standing in the shadows, his body sagging and dejected. Nok didn't have to ask to know what had happened.

Nok approached Trarck. "She's dead?"

Trarck nodded.

Melk, Cosk and Cleyed gathered around the two. Colonel Kairg immediately began questioning Trarck. "Where is her body? Do you think it was an accident or deliberate?" Kairg looked at Lydeck, who returned his gaze with a look that seemed all too knowing.

"Deliberate? As in she was murdered?" Trarck asked in disbelief.

Nok shared Trarck's disbelief. It was one thing to try and wrest power from another, but to go as far as murder? That would put them on par with the Royal Emperors. Nok held the Rockhoppers to a much higher standard than that. But still, Lydeck seemed to be reaching the same levels of ambition as Liutites lately. Nok stared down Lydeck, who appeared to be daring him to accuse him of Packt's murder.

Ki-ok approached Lydeck. The two glanced back toward Nok and walked away. After Ki-ok left, Nok started making connections. Why was Ki-ok suddenly so openly friendly with Lydeck? "Colonel Kairg," Nok said, his voice becoming that of Commander once again. "Packt was murdered."

"How can you know that?" Cosk asked. "Even Trarck can't say that with any certainty."

Nok looked to Trarck. "Where did you find her?"

"I found her on the rocks below the breach near her quarters. The petrels were already there."

Nok tried to shake the thought of her death from his mind. "What does your instinct tell you, Sergeant?"

Trarck hesitated, as if the future of the colony was resting on his answer. He finally let out a long breath. "I don't see how she could have fallen. It seems improbable that she would wander outside and trip."

"I feel the same way," Nok said. "Colonel Kairg, I want you to tail Lieutenant Ki-ok. I believe he may be in collusion with Lydeck and might have something to do with this. At the very least, he might know something."

Kairg clicked his beak together. "How about if I beat the information from him and save us the time and trouble?" Kairg answered his own question before Nok could enlighten him. "I know, I know, rule of law, squawk, squawk, squawk. It's all a load of guano when it comes to something like this. We know who the trouble is; we should eliminate the threat."

"As much as I would like to, we can't. Not yet. Lydeck hasn't *done* anything that we know of. And let us suppose at some point in the future somebody else disagrees with our ideals; do we just kill them too? No,

Kairg. It's a slippery rock to climb if we chose to do so. We have to trust the Tribunal, if and when it comes to that."

"If it does come to that, the damage might already be done." Kairg made his exit with a salute and a reassuring nod.

"Sergeant Trarck, call the Council to order. Before you protest, we have to inform the Council of Order of Packt's death. And then there is the Ministry of Defense and the Justice Tribunal—they will need to know." This wasn't the day Nok wanted. Today was supposed to have been a celebration of freedom, not a dive into a deeper sea of disaster.

After the usual opening rituals, Nok approached the center of the chamber. "It is with deep sadness that I must report the loss of our senior Council member, Packt. Her body was found moments ago. It appears as if she fell to her death. But we will know more after a full investigation." Nok glanced at Lydeck. Nok felt himself wish that Lydeck had been one of the many casualties of the war. The more he took on a smug air, the more Nok began to side with Kairg's way of thinking.

Nok shook away the thoughts and got to the business of the Council. "As much as I hate to do so, the first order of business will be finding a candidate to replace Packt's seat on the Council. I know this is all very sudden, but there are some important matters which need to be settled soon." He looked at Trarck who had noticed Ki-ok reenter the chamber and quietly stand next to Lydeck. "But first, I would like to hear from any members of the Council on this matter or any other." Nok was not surprised to see Lydeck take the opportunity to speak.

"Members of the Council, first let me say how deeply saddened I am to hear of our esteemed member's passing. She has left a void which I doubt will or can ever be filled. But while I do agree that our business must carry on, I am certain that at the very least, a brief recess is in order to give us all time to collect ourselves after this terrible tragedy." Lydeck finished by fixing Nok with a contemptuous and self-satisfied glare.

If Nok could have taken care of his Lydeck problem at that moment and gotten away with it, he might have. But Lydeck had played it well, and he had no choice but to call the Council to a brief recess. After watching his nemesis exit the room with Ki-ok in tow, he turned to Sergeant Trarck and the others. "Opinions, anyone?"

"For nominations?" Cosk asked.

"Yes. Packt was an ally, even though she didn't show it publicly. She almost always voted along our lines."

"If I may," Melk interrupted. "When did the Council turn factitious? Unity used to be our hallmark. Other colonies sought to emulate our strengths. And now, now we have nearly devolved back into the squabbling nest thieves which we were before Treeg sought a better way of life for us."

"It only takes one bad egg to bring the scavengers to the nest." Nok looked at Lydeck again. "We know about the egg, and now we need to find out who the scavengers are."

"But before we go on a scavenger hunt, we need to decide who we will nominate to replace Packt," Cleyed said from outside the circle of Rockhoppers.

"In this current climate I can't think of anyone that I would want to upset for nominating them," Cosk said, looking at Trarck.

Melk began bouncing with impatience as he waited his turn to speak. "What about Seck?" he asked, not caring how his impropriety might seem to the others.

Nok studied Melk for a moment, and when Melk was close to apologizing, he spoke. "That's a very good suggestion."

"Thank you, sir. I am certain that she would appreciate the opportunity to serve. After all, she did secede her nomination for Council to me. To which I am eternally grateful. And the fact that she is one of the three living survivors of whom you took part in liberating from that awful human vessel, Commander Nok; which is not to discount Tog, brave Rockhopper he was, giving his life in the fight against that dreadful General Diutes. Which leaves only myself, her, and Lydeck of that group of four. And I think it would be most conscionable of us to—"

"Melk," Nok interrupted. "None of us disagree with you. She's a perfect choice. In fact I think we should inform her and ask her if this is what she wants. Are you coming with us?"

It took Melk a couple of seconds before he realized what Nok had said. Without further verbosity, he led the way to Seck's chamber.

CHAPTER 32

Lydeck crept toward the darkest part of the central warren, not daring to take the risk of going to the lower passages. He stopped and listened to the breath of Ki-ok coming from the back of the dead-end passage.

"Were you followed?"

"I've been doing this long enough to know how not to be seen, lieutenant. The real question is, were you able to lose Colonel Kairg? It was foolish of you to come into the Council chamber as you did. Did you see the way Nok looked at you? He suspects something." With no light in the passage Lydeck, could hear instead of see Ki-ok's anger rise. He braced himself for another spat of babbling repetition. What he got instead was an unexpected curt reply.

"If he suspects me, then I will make sure that he suspects you as well, Lydeck." It was as forceful as Ki-ok had ever been.

Lydeck took a step back. Something had changed in Ki-ok. Perhaps killing the old Rockhopper gave him a boost of unwarranted self-confidence. He made a mental note to have Ki-ok killed before long. Lydeck readied himself to harangue Ki-ok's new found confidence, but was interrupted by a voice that had gotten far too close without notice.

"They have put me in charge of security of the crèche."

Lydeck turned toward the voice. "You're serious? Tell me you're serious."

"I am. I would suggest that you get to doing what you are going to do very soon."

Lydeck closed what distance remained between them. "Tretak, my dear, as much as I would like to, I can't at this moment. The Council will be returning from recess and we will be voting on a new member. So perhaps it would be best if you take care of it."

"Why do they need a new Council member? And who are you going to nominate?" Tretak asked, ignoring his suggestion.

Lydeck paused. "Our esteemed Council member Packt met with an unfortunate accident. Didn't she, Ki-ok?" Ki-ok didn't answer. "As far as a viable candidate, I have Trasik-lon taking care of that."

"Nominate me," Tretak said. "What better way to put sand in Kairg's mouth that to put me on the Council."

"Interesting. But while I like the way you think, you don't have the experience. The Council of Order can be an ordeal—a daily battle, to say the least."

"I've been in a few battles myself. And who on the Council had any experience prior to it being formed by General Treeg?"

Lydeck considered his options. The more he thought it over, the more he liked the idea of slapping Nok in the face with a Rockhopper he had trusted. It could work, but he would have to work fast. "Very well, Council member Tretak, we'll do it. I am certain that we have the vote to pull it off. But we have to move quickly on the other end. Once you're exposed, they will rush to the crèche. Leeg will have to be gone by then. Which reminds me—where is Keerka? She always has her beak in Council business."

"She went in search of Kicki and hasn't been seen since."

Lydeck pondered the information. "That could be good or bad news. The good would be that my shadowy friends deep in the warren found her and killed her. The bad would be that she found them and is on her way to tell Nok. Either way, we need to get this vote done immediately. I have it on good accord that our less than illustrious leader is about to step down as Commander. So now we only need to eliminate Nok from the equation and show him what meddling in my business brings upon him. And that's where you come in, Ki-ok."

Ki-ok's claws could be heard scratching against the stone. "Me? You want me to kill Commander Nok? Pushing old penguins off a cliff is one thing, but I doubt I can do the same to an experienced warrior such as him. However, I should be able to take care of a penguin with less combat skill without a problem."

Ki-ok's emotionless tone briefly unsettled Lydeck. His trademark nervous demeanor had all but disappeared, and he spoke with the voice of someone who had lost all good humor, someone who wouldn't hesitate to kill a penguin who attempted to betray him.

"No, my War Chief. Not Commander Nok. He is, unfortunately, untouchable at the moment. But his son isn't. Before you protest, you won't have to do the deed. Just take him below to the friends I spoke of and they will take care of it."

Lydeck sensed Ki-ok's hesitation. "Nok will become a nonfactor once this is done. But time is of the essence; once Tretak is presented as a candidate for the Council, they will rush to the crèche. Go now. Move quickly, my friend."

Ki-ok left without saying another word. After he was gone, it was Tretak's turn to speak. "Who are your friends?"

Lydeck didn't like the accusation in her voice. "Nobody you should be concerned about at the moment. I have to get back to the Council. Wait until the nominations have been called for before you enter. We can't show them our intentions too soon. And Tretak, you're in this too deep to have second thoughts now. Don't make me regret my decision."

Tretak waited until Lydeck was gone before following after. She scanned the corridors and spotted Lydeck's crest bouncing as he headed toward the Council chamber. "Oh, my *dear* Lydeck, you won't live long enough to have any regrets."

CHAPTER 33

Commander Nok stood on the dais and let out a heavy breath. He looked out at the Council of Order with a melancholy emptiness. When General Treeg had first formed the Ministry, and later the Council of Order and Tribunal, the Rockhoppers were filled with hope for a united and peaceful future. But Nok realized that it was Treeg's fierce determination and air of strength and power that had held it together. Treeg had only his hope of a better life for all to push him and never let him lose sight of the goal. Nok also realized that he lacked that strength of will. The war had stolen it from him, and because of that, the Rockhopper Defense Ministry and its accordant bodies were crumbling.

Of all of the Rockhoppers he knew, only two were capable of reuniting the colony. One was Keerka. Her strength far outshone Nok's own and her determination was unmatched by any Rockhopper. But she would never want to enter the whirlpool of discord that the Council had become. That left Trarck; brave, intelligent, and with enough internal strength that even the brash Colonel Kairg would submit to him without a second thought. Trarck was the penguin the Rockhoppers needed.

"I call the Council from recess, with business resuming as ordered." Nok circled the dais, gathering his thoughts. "I had originally intended for only one motion to be presented today. But with the unexpected passing of Packt, we will have two votes presented to the Order." None of the Rockhoppers stirred at hearing about a second vote, which told Nok that his carefully guarded secret about his resignation was not as carefully guarded as he had thought.

"Since the second election cannot be completed without the first, we will be voting on Packt's replacement." Nok hesitated, fully expecting Lydeck to raise an objection. When there were none forthcoming, he felt his melancholy transform into a burgeoning dread.

"Commander, may we know the nature of the second vote? I can hardly vote for the first knowing the second is so dependent on its outcome." Lydeck looked to Kank, Trasik-lon, and Kerl who were vigorously nodding their heads in agreement.

Nok looked to Trarck, who gave him a barely perceptible shake of his head. Nok leaned into Trarck to hear his objections.

"Commander, I wouldn't reveal your motives just yet. Lydeck is up to something. What it is, I don't know."

"Lydeck is always up to something. I say we call him on it and force him to step off the nest and show his eggs," Nok replied in a whisper.

"You know the Council rules better than me, sir. But if you present it, they will insist it become a motion," Trarck said, never taking his eyes off of Lydeck. "I don't think it would be wise."

Nok considered his options. It was easier when the only risks he assumed involved him. The personal choice to assist Lavour, Leepoh and Meuseaux in bringing down Liutites was easy compared to this, but it was one that ultimately cost Leepoh his life. And as they always seemed to do, his thoughts fell back on his friend. "What I wouldn't give to hear that Gentoo's blathering right now. He'd probably be telling me about some great squid hunt instead of actually helping me. But I have to focus on the here and now." He looked to the sergeant. "I'll call his bluff." Trarck closed his eyes as Nok turned his attention back to the Council.

"I was hoping to do this under better circumstances, but since you ask, Council member Lydeck. I intend to step down as Commander and nominate Sergeant Trarck as my replacement." Nok braced himself for the elevated chattering the announcement would cause, but was disappointed by the lack thereof.

"I must say this is a surprise, Commander Nok. But I can see that you have the best interest of the colony in mind, and for that I commend you," Lydeck said with unusual courtesy. "But if I may ask, is this a formal motion or a…oh I don't know, a declaration of intent?"

Nok cringed. Trarck had been right. Lydeck, for whatever reason was hoping for this. "Neither, Lydeck. It was just a statement in casual conversation," he said, hoping Lydeck would take it as such. But he knew better.

"A casual conversation? As you and I both know, such declarations, when presented to this assembly while in session, especially by the Commander, are to be considered either a motion or declaration. There are no casual conversations during an open forum. Are you telling me that you intend to circumnavigate the rules which govern this body? And if so, should this be a matter brought before the Tribunal?" Lydeck stood self-satisfied as the Council erupted into open squabbling.

Nok glared at Lydeck. It wasn't a complete disaster; at least he was prying open the shell of Lydeck's intentions. "No, Council member Lydeck," Nok said with a cheerfulness he did not feel. He looked around as the chamber quieted. "You can consider it a formal motion to be brought for the vote after we choose our new Council of Order member."

"Very well, Commander. I will look forward to the election." Lydeck resumed his relaxed stance.

"But before we proceed, can you tell me, Council member Lydeck, why you have disobeyed the Commander's direct edict? I see all of the other representatives have their apprentices with them; where is yours?"

Lydeck stood. "He has chosen to resign his position."

"Ah, I see. I have heard the contrary. I believe an investigation is in order, after which it will be brought before the Tribunal for judgment."

Lydeck glared at Nok. "You wouldn't dare."

"I do dare, Lydeck. As my final order as Commander I am assigning an investigation committee to look into the matter. The committee will consist of Cosk, Melk, and Trasik-lon, and they will report directly to the Tribunal." Nok looked at Trarck, who returned a surprised, yet satisfied look. He returned his gaze toward Lydeck and noticed his demeanor had shifted from arrogance to outright anger. "Now that that is settled, we will be taking nominations for Council."

Melk stood first. "I would like to formally nominate Seck for Council. Her devotion to the betterment of the colony is unsurpassed. In fact, as many of you know, it was she who withdrew her candidacy to allow room for me. It is that unselfishness which exemplifies her core strengths as a Rockhopper who puts the elevation and well-being of others before herself. And I believe, and I am certain that not a single Rockhopper can deny this, that she can and will make for a fine Council member."

"Thank you, Melk," Nok said before the other could take another breath and continue. "Let's keep the personal remarks to a minimum for now. Is there a second?" Cosk seconded the nomination and Seck entered the chamber, taking her place to the side of Commander Nok. "Are there any other nominations?"

"Yes, Commander Nok," Lydeck said as he stood. His cockiness had returned nearly as fast as it had left. "I would like to nominate Tretak."

"Tretak?" He admitted that he barely knew her, but she had been so well vouched for by Melk and Kairg. Lydeck had done it. He outsmarted, outwitted and outplayed him at every turn. Now matters were worse. If Trasik-lon, Kerl, and Kank voted with Lydeck, and he was certain they would, the opposition would hold the majority. The Commander's vote was only used for tie-breakers. As his mind spun between berating himself for not listening to Trarck and seeing what little vestige of Treeg's dream crumble, a thought occurred to him. Tretak was supposed to be guarding the crèche. "Who has taken your place at the crèche, Tretak?" The anger in

Nok's voice was apparent.

"No one to my knowledge, Commander. I felt that this took precedence over a minor security detail," Tretak said casually.

"I don't know what Lydeck has promised you, but if any harm comes to any fledgling in the crèche, I promise you that I will see you brought before the Tribunal and tried for treason. This session is adjourned."

"Commander Nok, We have two elective motions on the floor. The edicts of this Council clearly state that any motions on the floor must be voted upon before adjournment. As you have threatened my candidate, you yourself might be brought before the Tribunal for dereliction of your elected duties. Is that what you want your *final* act as Commander of the Council of Order to be?"

Again, Lydeck's air was smug to the point of pleading to be severely beaten. But Nok wouldn't take this bait. "Very well. All those in favor of Seck as Council member, say *so*."

"So," Melk, Cleyed and Cosk said in unison.

Nok let out a sigh of disgust. Trasik-lon was firmly in Lydeck's camp. "All those in favor of Tretak as Council member, say *so*." As expected, Lydeck, Trasik-lon, Kank, and Kerl elected Tretak. "Congratulations, Tretak, you are now a member of the Council of Order within the Rockhopper Defense Ministry." Nok wasted no time in finding out what he already knew would happen. He called for the election of Trarck as Commander, to which Kerl nominated Lydeck. Within a minute Lydeck was elected as Commander.

Lydeck let out a squawk of victory and headed toward the dais.

"Not so fast, Commander elect. You do not take your position until this meeting is adjourned. I now call this meeting," Nok looked to his friends on the Council and lowered his head, "to recess." He hoped off of the dais. Along with Trarck, Seck, and the others, he rushed out of the chamber, listening to Lydeck's calls of shenanigans disappear behind him.

CHAPTER 34

Kicki urged Keerka to move. After killing the Shadow Warrior, the two had made their way up the passage, but the beating Keerka took had taken its toll. Her head felt as if it were caught in a rip tide and her legs became too weak to carry her. "Kicki, sweetie. Give me a moment. I just need to get my strength back."

"But Miss Keerka…," Kicki had seen more of what might come. The Seeing had become part of consciousness. In a span of only a few minutes, it had gone from coming to her as if she were dreaming, to melding with the here and now. And what she saw worried her. She wanted to tell Keerka of the danger that Leeg was still in, but she also knew what would happen if she did. "I have to get Commander Nok…now."

Keerka waited before answering, caught in the dilemma of putting trust in her youthful inexperience or trusting in her proven ability. "Go. I'll be here. Be careful, be quick."

Kicki hesitated, nodded and scampered away. After only a few steps, she turned around and ran back to Keerka. "Stop Ki-ok if you can. Do not trust him."

"Lieutenant Ki-ok?" Keerka started to get to her feet. "What has he got to do with this?"

She saw the varying waves of what might be, and on every crest but one, Nok died. Her heart ached for Keerka as she searched for the path to saving Nok's life. When she found it, she did not like what had to be done. "Ki-ok is the same as Lydeck…or worse. Stay where you are. If you move now, Leeg's life will be lost." Kicki looked at Keerka without seeing her. Her words reverberated off of the stone, but the echo changed what she heard. The words were the same but with different meanings. Ghosts of what could happen walked alongside of what was happening. The present was catching up with the future. And she had to do what she could to ensure the best possible future became the present. Before they all became the past.

Keerka saw Kicki's eyes in the gloom. They were wide, catching glimmers of the vague light streaming from the upper passage. "Kicki, don't be afraid. Leeg will be all right."

Kicki knew the adult was trying to ease her fears. But she realized that she wasn't afraid. Fear had left her. All she felt now were the possible heartbreaks and joys of what would or could be. She walked through the shadows, forms dashed in and out of existence; they surrounded her but could not see her.

Understanding gripped her. The future will never be determined with any certainty; by her simply existing, or as long as an Oracle lived, the future could never be set. She also knew that the frightening penguin she had seen in her vision would come for her. He was the thief of the future, and he would kill her to ensure that future. She turned away and fled the corridor. She knew that she would soon have to flee the colony, if only to ensure their survival. Aperion would come for her eventually, but first, she had to save Lydeck.

CHAPTER 35

Ki-ok pushed Leeg toward the entry to the crèche, but the young Rockhopper couldn't pull his eyes off of Eeco. Her dead eyes seemed to be looking back at him, as if apologizing for failing to protect the crèche. The fledglings were huddled in the corner, paralyzed by fear of having one of their own kill the old female. She had done what she could, but Ki-ok would not be stopped, adding a second old female to his list of murders. Leeg knew he would be next. Ki-ok had told him either now or later and Leeg chose later. Another sharp jab of a beak to his back, and Leeg did as he was instructed.

Leeg silently thanked the Ancients that Kicki had been gone; otherwise she would have done what she could to stop this Rockhopper, and she would have been killed as well. Ki-ok pushed him through one of the passageways to the lower levels. For an area that he knew was usually off-limits to most penguins, it had become quite busy over the past couple of days. They clambered over a small rock formation and Leeg tumbled over the other side.

"Get up. Quit stalling," Ki-ok said, his voice just above a whisper.

Leeg got to his feet and stalled some more. "I'm not stalling, sir. I'm not very good at climbing just yet."

A slap of a flipper to his head sent him back to the ground. "You are stalling. Now move it." Ki-ok looked around as if he heard something.

When it appeared that he hadn't, he pushed Leeg to his feet once again.

The slightest of movement in the shadows caught Leeg's eye as he stood. His heart thumped when he saw who it was. It was Kicki. He kept his eye on her for a fraction of a heartbeat, hoping that she would stay where she was. When she didn't move, he felt a twinge of betrayal. He didn't want her to risk her life for him, but he was certain that she would. He walked forward, stealing one last glance back toward her, but she was nowhere to be seen. "Good," he said in his quietest voice. Hopefully she had a plan. She was the smartest penguin he knew, even if she was the youngest. Feeling a little more confident, he moved forward on his own accord.

The light began to fade behind them as they worked their way deeper down the passages. Leeg stumbled and fell, letting out a loud whimper when he hit the ground again.

"Get to your feet," Ki-ok ordered. "How the Commander could sire such a clumsy offspring is beyond my reasoning."

"I'm sorry, sir. I'm not clumsy, it's just very dark and I—"

"Shut up. No more excuses. If you slow me down again, I might decide that it would be better to just knock you unconscious and drag you down there."

"And where will you be dragging my son to, Lieutenant Ki-ok?"

Leeg was at once elated to hear his mother's voice and scared by the venom it carried. He pulled away and he ran to Keerka's side. She gave him a reassuring nudge with her flipper and he scooted in behind her. Now things were different. It was about to become a very bad day for Ki-ok. Leeg understood why Kicki had left. She knew Keerka was here and waiting for them. He pressed in close to his mother, but when he did he felt her unsteadiness. Her body seemed to be swaying and trembling as if she were having a difficult time standing. He wanted to ask if she was all right, but with Ki-ok standing nearby, he knew better.

"Keerka?" The confidence in Ki-ok's voice melted away. "I was simply taking him to a safer place. Much safer. Lydeck plans to have the boy killed.

Killed. In fact, he thinks I am in support of his taking over the Council. I'm not. I assure you I am not. That's why I am moving your son. I'm just moving him to a safer place."

"It seems that both you and Lydeck only have my son's best interest in mind when you kidnap him." Keerka took a shaky step forward. She leaned close to Leeg. "Is this true, son?"

Leeg looked at the silhouetted form of Ki-ok. "He killed Eeco, the crèche minder. He killed her in front of all of us."

Keerka turned her gaze back to Ki-ok, her body tense and ready. "And murdering an old Rockhopper is the best way to ensure my son's protection?"

Ki-ok stayed silent for a moment. Leeg could see him swelling from submissive to aggressive against the backdrop of dim light. "Stupid fledgling. You should have stayed quiet. Now I'll have to kill your mother as well."

Keerka told Leeg to run. As he tried to slip past Ki-ok he was met with a slap of his flipper. Leeg tumbled backwards, finally coming to rest at Keerka's feet. "I'm sorry, mother. I guess I zagged when I shouldn't have gone that way at all," he said, quoting his father, who usually quoted Leepoh. His head flopped backwards, and suddenly, all he wanted to do was sleep.

∧∧∧

Hatred brimmed in Keerka's eyes as she stepped toward her opponent. "Before I kill you, you are going to tell me everything you know about Lydeck." The adrenaline of an impending fight buoyed her strength, but she still felt like she was standing on a wave.

"Keerka, do you honestly think I would tell you that? I can tell by the quiver in your voice that you are injured. I was hoping not to have to kill you in front of your son, but if you continue this course of action, you will leave me no choice."

Keerka landed her first hit as soon as Ki-ok finished his taunt, aiming for his throat. She had to settle for a gash on his breast.

Ki-ok stayed on his feet. He reacted before Keerka could get in a second strike, leaping straight at her with both feet extended forward. The impact knocked Keerka to her back, but Ki-ok's momentum sent him flailing over her body. He tried to get to her and land a killing strike, but she was on her feet and ready to attack.

The two Rockhoppers circled each other in the darkness, eyes wide and ready. "It's true—you don't fight like an old penguin. But even if you manage to beat me, I guarantee that the end will come soon enough for you and your mate."

"Well then, it's a shame that you won't live to see that."

"You and your mate really are fools. Lydeck has been making alliances with the Royals to end your rule. Through it all, this entire time, you've had no idea. It's really quite pathetic how the enemy stood right underneath your beaks and you didn't have even the slightest clue."

Keerka's head felt like it was caught in a whirlpool, and had to brace herself against a rock. "I know all about your master's alliance with the Royals, Ki-ok. In fact, I just killed a Shadow Warrior moments before you arrived. They put up a good fight, but they die just like any other creature."

"You lie," Ki-ok spat out. "Even the mighty Keerka could not kill one of those monsters alone."

"No? Perhaps you should take a look for yourself. Its corpse is in the passage you're headed to."

Ki-ok snickered. "A good effort on your part—trying to delay while you recover and hope for your mate to arrive and save you. But time is wasting and now I have to kill you." He rushed Keerka, slapping with his flippers and stabbing.

Keerka blocked the pecks with her own beak, trying to land the occasional peck herself. But she didn't have the strength to block the winged attack. Slap after slap landed, and soon her stamina began to wane. Ki-ok struck harder and harder. His beak found its mark against her chest sending Keerka floundering to the ground.

"Now," Ki-ok panted, "I am sorry, but I have to kill you. Who am I kidding—I'm not sorry in the least."

CHAPTER 36

"No!" Leeg screamed, rushing in at Ki-ok. He hit the older Rockhopper with enough force to make him take a step back.

Ki-ok looked down at his fuzzy attacker. "You have your mother's bravery and your father's stupidity."

Leeg reared back and jabbed his beak into Ki-ok's stomach. The next thing he knew, he was flying through the air. He cringed just before he hit the rock floor and watched the world tumble around as he rolled to a stop. It took a moment for him to get his bearings and when he did he could just make out the outline of Ki-ok standing over his mother.

He had to get to her. He would save her no matter what. He tried to stand, but his legs wouldn't cooperate. He crawled forward at first until his legs found their strength. "You will not kill my mother!"

Leeg charged at Ki-ok once more. Ki-ok slapped him to the ground. His strength was gone, but his determination hadn't changed. He got to his feet once more and fell into Ki-ok's side with his beak.

"Will you stay down!" Ki-ok shouted. He beat Leeg until he was certain he wouldn't get up again.

Leeg's eyes fell shut and he heard Ki-ok mutter something about killing him next. He braced himself and waited to hear his mother cry out when Ki-ok killed her. He had done what he could. But the sound didn't come.

Instead, he swore he heard Kicki say something about Commander Nok. Joy filled his heart. His father was coming, and soon he would take care of Ki-ok and save him and his mother. Then he heard the sound of clawed feet slapping against stone. Something struck him on the head, which was followed by a sharp pain in his right flipper. He felt as if he were in the air, swaying back and forth on an invisible wave. And then he felt nothing.

CHAPTER 37

Kicki ran toward the Council chamber. She didn't need to stop at the crèche; she already knew what she would find there. As she neared the chamber, she spotted Ki-ok duck out of a dark cave. She waited. Soon after Lydeck followed. Kicki started to head toward the chamber when she saw Tretak exit the cave as well. She jumped back into the shadows and watched her. She was headed for the Council chamber as well. She hadn't seen Tretak as an accomplice to Lydeck.

There were no scenarios she had seen where Tretak had any role in helping Lydeck. On top of that, seeing Ki-ok didn't make sense. He had already killed Eeco; he shouldn't be here. Kicki's eyes went wide. She wasn't seeing the present or the future. She was seeing the past. Shadows of recent events were whispering to her, directing her toward the future.

Kicki leaned against the wall and dragged her feet across the well-worn pathway, her claws clicking in grooves created by centuries of Rockhopper feet on the stone. She closed her eyes to block out the present and past to see where the waves would take her. The future was as fluid as the sea, and she was just beginning to understand. She wouldn't be able to see it all; and she now knew that there are those you can save and those who must die. Her mind's eye split into countless fractal pieces and she saw what needed to be done. Why hadn't she seen it before? Did her choosing this path lead to what might happen? It was all too much for such a young mind to comprehend. What she did know was that she had to get back to Keerka immediately.

She turned to run and bumped squarely into Colonel Kairg's belly. "Where are you off to in such a hurry, little one?"

"Excuse me, sir, but I have to go." She stared up at Kairg, again wondering why she hadn't known he would be there. Earlier in the day, she had known every move the Shadow Warrior would make. But now she only saw the larger possibilities. Maybe it was a matter of focus. If she focused too much on what would come later, she couldn't see what was about to happen.

"Now, you just wait a minute. Where are your parents? Commander Nok has declared martial law. All Rockhoppers are supposed to be at their roosts. Now let's get you there."

"But Nok is no longer Commander. How can he make declarations?" She didn't know why she had asked that, only that she had to.

Colonel Kairg stooped down to eye level with Kicki. "You're speaking beyond your years." He paused. "Most penguins don't know that yet. But we need to keep it that way for just a little bit longer. Now, my little eavesdropper, can you do that?"

Kicki stared at the colonel and felt her body rock as the Seeing told her the possibilities. "Yes, sir. I can keep it that way. I need your help, though." She realized that Kairg was staring at her with a perplexed look as he watched her odd gyrations.

"I haven't much time, but what do you need help—wait, you're Kicki. We were about to send a search party."

"Ki-ok has killed Eeco and taken Leeg. You need to tell Nok. And whatever you do, don't let him kill Lydeck. He can't kill him. If only for Leeg's sake, he can't."

"Ki-ok? Where is he? Nok will have my head plumes for losing him."

"Just get Commander Nok and your search party. Keerka is in danger."

"Right. Where did Ki-ok take Leeg?"

"To the lower levels. Ki-ok plans to have the Shadow Warriors kill him for Lydeck."

Colonel Kairg stared wide-eyed at the youthful Rockhopper. "Oh, Nok won't kill Lydeck; I will kill him myself."

"No, it must be Tretak, or better yet, no one at all," Kicki said as she ran down the corridor. "Get Commander Nok now!"

"Tretak is Lydeck's co-conspirator. She has already betrayed us," Kairg said to himself as he watched Kicki disappear around a corner.

Kicki popped her head back around the corner. "She is only providing him with a large enough ballast stone to choke himself."

Kicki ran back to the passage to the lower levels and leaned against the entryway while staying out of sight. She could hear the scuffle between Keerka and Ki-ok, and knew that Keerka was not faring well against the lieutenant. There was little she could do to help, and the Seeing had only shown Keerka dying under Ki-ok's beak. An idea popped into her head and immediately the visions changed.

Kicki steadied her nerves as best she could. New shadows swirled before her, each taking divergent paths, some showing her own death where she stood. She stepped into clearing, her form silhouetted by the pale light. "He's down here, Commander Nok." She waited and then she heard Ki-ok mutter something followed by an abbreviated cry from Leeg.

Kicki held her breath, stepped back, and waited. She didn't know if Ki-ok was headed toward her, running off alone, or was with Leeg; or he could be killing both Keerka and Leeg; all of the shadows were still in play. All but one disappeared. She had saved Keerka. There was more to be done, but she couldn't be everywhere at one time. And she knew that the adults wouldn't believe her if she explained how she knew what she did. She allowed herself to fall into the Seeing. The shadows of what had been and what was to come began to swirl around her with such speed that it was all she could do to catch sight of them. Through it all, she found the answer to her next question, even though all signs showed her he wouldn't help.

CHAPTER 38

Colonel Kairg rushed into the crèche to find Nok and Trarck standing over the body of Eeco. Melk, Seck, Cosk, and Cleyed tended to the young fear-stricken Rockhoppers. "Commander Nok, sir," he said with his eyes cast downward.

Nok spun and cast angry accusatory eyes on Kairg. "It is just Nok now, Colonel."

Kairg hesitated before replying. "You are still *my* commander."

Nok's eyes were filled with venom and fear. His voice quivered when he spoke. "It's all irrelevant. I have to find Leeg. That's all that matters now. I've sent a patrol to bring me Tretak. Her betrayal has cost me my son. And then I will hunt down and kill Lydeck like I should have long before now."

Kairg lifted his head and took a deep breath. "This is my fault, Commander. Ki-ok did this, or so I've been told. I lost him. It was he who took Leeg and he killed Eeco. I will resign my post as soon as we settle this."

Ever the level-headed one, Trarck jumped in the conversation. "At least now we know who murdered Packt. When we catch him, he will be brought up on charges."

"We don't have time for further conversation," Kairg said. "I know which way Ki-ok went. He went to the lower levels. If we hurry, we can catch them."

Nok looked at Kairg, then turned to the others. "Melk, you and Seck get the young ones to their parents. The rest of you are with us." He ran out of the crèche before Melk could reply. "Tell me Colonel, where are you getting your information?"

"One of the fledglings, sir…Kicki. She's safe and she was near the Council chamber when I went—"

Nok skidded to a halt. "Kicki? What did she say?"

"Mostly just what I've told you. She was acting odd, though…kind of spooky, if you ask me. She said that Lydeck has allied himself with Shadow Warriors and that you mustn't kill Lydeck."

Nok let out an exasperated breath. "Do you believe her about the Shadow Warriors?"

Kairg looked at the others who had gathered around them. "Yes sir. However odd her behavior, I could tell that was being forthright. She also said that Tretak is the only one who can kill Lydeck. Not you, not me, just Tretak."

"Tretak? She's next on my list of traitors. And I *will* kill Lydeck. I promise you that."

"She said something about Tretak letting Lydeck choke himself on a stone. I'm not sure how she came to this information; I can only assume that she overheard a conversation somehow."

"Regardless of how, we now know Lydeck is behind the murders and he has put my son in danger. For that, I will kill him."

Nok began to stomp away but Trarck stopped him. "Sir, Kicki is right. You can't kill Lydeck. None of us can."

"I can and I will, Sergeant."

Trarck looked his longtime friend in the eye. "No you can't. Lydeck is the Commander elect. If you kill him, you will be brought before the Tribunal and sentenced to death. It's the law; there can be no exceptions. You know this."

Nok was about to argue more before Kairg stopped him. "There's more, sir. She said Keerka is in danger."

Nok stared at Kairg through frightened but determined eyes. He wouldn't lose his entire family in one day. He couldn't. He had been through it before and he refused to go through it again. "I will do what it takes to save my family. And if that means I am brought before the Tribunal…so be it." He darted down the path before the others could stop him.

"We have to protect him," Trarck said.

Kairg returned the other's gaze. "We will, Sergeant. *We* will do whatever it takes. Gather the forces. I have a feeling this may result in a fight. The Tribunal cannot charge Nok if we are in the midst of a civil war."

"Is that an order, sir?" Trarck asked, his voice low.

Kairg hesitated. "Yes, Sergeant Trarck. I will take responsibility for any actions not deemed legal while you are under my command." Trarck lifted his beak in a salute and hustled off with Colonel Kairg watching him. "Provided we are the victors."

CHAPTER 39

"Tearsk…Tearsk," Kicki called into the dark chamber. "Tearsk. I know you're in there."

"Leave me alone Kicki."

Kicki paced around the entrance. Her patience with Tearsk was ebbing. "Will you come out of there? I need your help. If you don't come out, I'm coming in." She heard the slap of penguin feet against stone and backed away.

"Go away. Just go away. I don't want to help you. I don't want to help anybody."

"Why are you hiding in this stupid cave?" Kicki snapped. "If you help me, Rockhoppers everywhere will know you as the penguin who saved RHC23."

Tearsk gave Kicki a look of disdain and headed back down the cave.

The Seeing was giving Kicki nothing at the moment. Kicki decided that she still had her wits, and that was something she knew she could use on Tearsk. "There's a chance to get back at Lydeck." Satisfaction set in when she heard Tearsk's feet stop slapping.

"I hate Lydeck. I don't ever want to see him again." His voice was filled with spite, but at least he wasn't walking away any longer.

"After what he said to you and your parents, I would think you want a chance to knock him down a few stones." Kicki tried not to congratulate herself just yet. Her plan was working, but she didn't have him yet. Even though she hadn't seen the faintest shadow in several minutes, she knew time was running out.

"How do you know what Lydeck said?" Tearsk demanded, stomping closer to Kicki.

"The son of the Commander *is* my best friend, you know. Nothing gets past Commander Nok." Tearsk didn't say anything. "Come on. You know you want to get back at that spineless little Skua."

After several moments Tearsk stepped closer to Kicki. "What can *I* do to Lydeck? I'm nothing. I'm sure if I do anything, I'll just mess it up."

"You won't. You can't. It's really simple. And if you do it, all of Lydeck's scheming will come crashing down and the whole colony will know you took part in it." The latter part was a lie. Kicki had no idea who would think what, but she was sure as the sea going to do her best to see that Tearsk got his recognition. He was a real pain in the tail-feathers, but she hated to see his spirit broken so badly. "If you're going to help, you need to decide now. We're running out of time."

Tearsk looked at Kicki, his beak parted to speak. He looked away and let out a heavy breath. "Figure it out for yourself and just leave me alone." He turned and hurried back to the darkest part of the cave.

She had to figure out what to do. She tried to summon her ability, but could only get vague wisps of forms that she didn't understand. She began her long, dejected walk back toward where she had last seen Keerka when a voice stopped her.

"You know all penguins are supposed to be restricted to their roost, don't you, little one?"

Kicki spun around and saw Tretak standing not two meters away. "I'm sorry, ma'am. I hadn't heard." There was no reply. Instead Tretak continued to talk to another Rockhopper chick. Tretak and the unknown chick walked down the corridor, laughing and talking. Whoever the chick was, she wasn't in trouble. Kicki followed and saw Tretak playfully race the chick further down the path. Kicki rushed to catch them as they rounded a corner. When she rounded the corner she saw Tretak guide the chick inside of a chamber. Tretak stopped, looked back at Kicki, and fell away like sand carried on a gale. Kicki shuddered. "What in the Great Sea was that?"

"What was what?" a voice came from behind, making Kicki jump.

"Tearsk?" Kicki tapped him with her flipper to make sure he was real. "Does this mean you're going to help?"

"I really hate that penguin." He looked up and down the abandoned corridor. "Who were you talking to?"

Still feeling more than a little troubled, Kicki led Tearsk away at a brisk pace. "No one. I just thought I saw somebody, I was wrong."

"Hmm, whatever you say," Tearsk said, eyeing Kicki suspiciously. "Now, what am I supposed to do to keep Lydeck from doing whatever it is he's doing?"

CHAPTER 40

Nok ran along the rough stone tunnel with the intention of killing everything that crossed his path. He had had his fill of fighting and war, but no matter what he did, or how hard he tried, it seemed to pursue him like a leopard seal hunting its quarry. Now he was forced to fight again. He didn't care what the Tribunal, Kicki or Trarck had to say; he was going to kill Lydeck and kill Ki-ok. And if there really were Shadow Warriors down there, he would kill them too. Lost in his rage, he nearly tripped over Keerka.

"Nok," Keerka said, her voice just above a whisper. "You need to watch where you're going. You never know what you might stumble upon down here."

Nok was by her side in an instant. "Keerka. What are you doing down here? What happened? Are you all right? Can you stand?"

Keerka tried to stand, but her head still protested the effort, and she slid down against a rock. "Slow down seal wrangler. Let me answer one question before you ask the next."

Nok rested his beak against hers, trying to reassure her that she would be all right.

"I went down here searching for Kicki. I found her, but I found a lot more. Nok, there are Royal Emperors here...Shadow Warriors."

Nok looked at Kairg, who had just arrived. "It seems as if Kicki has her beak in everything at the moment." Kairg nodded.

"There's more to her than you know, but I'll tell you later. Long story short, I confronted a Shadow Warrior. Its body is a little further down the path, but it knocked me around pretty good." Keerka's mood became as dark as her surroundings. "Nok, Ki-ok has our son. He means to hurt him. He must be stopped."

"Commander," Kairg said. "Let me track him down. I'll take care of Ki-ok, you see to Keerka's safety. Cleyed, Cosk and I can handle Ki-ok—if they haven't gotten too soft from sitting on the Council, that is."

"I'll show you who's soft, Colonel," Cleyed said.

"That's out of the question, Colonel," Keerka said as she tried to stand again.

"Keerka, Nok is no longer Commander. Lydeck is. And if Nok kills either Lydeck or Ki-ok, he will be brought before the Tribunal and summarily executed. We can't allow that."

"I don't care. I have to get our son," Nok pleaded. "I have to."

"No you don't," Keerka said. "You'll be distracted with worry for me, and distractions are dangerous. Let Kairg take Ki-ok. Have Ki-ok stand trial for his actions."

"He killed Packt and Eeco. I don't think he will hesitate to kill Leeg." If there was anybody who could make Nok see reason it was his mate. She was just as volatile as him, but slightly less impulsive. He stood and faced Kairg, finally relenting. "Find our son. Take whatever measures necessary in apprehending Ki-ok. If he resists, you know what you have to do. Now, what about the Shadow Warriors? For all we know, there could be any number of Royals down there."

"Sergeant Trarck is taking care of that, sir. I promise you, I will get your son back safely and I *will* make Ki-ok pay, one way or another."

"Are sure this is the best course of action?" Nok said to his mate.

"Stay with me. I need your help and we have a lot to talk about. I trust Colonel Kairg. Between him, Cleyed, and Cosk, I'm certain they can handle this."

"You heard her, Colonel." Nok sat beside Keerka and watched the vague forms of his friends disappear. Once he no longer heard them, he turned his full attention back toward Keerka. "Now tell me, how badly are you injured?"

"It's not bad. I hit my head during the scuffle with the Royal."

"It could have been much worse. I don't know how you managed to kill a Shadow Warrior, but you never cease to amaze me."

"I wish I could take all of the credit, but if it wasn't for Kicki, I doubt I would have survived. She is a remarkable penguin, Nok. She's clever and brave beyond her years. In fact, I only came down searching for her because she was looking for Leeg. Those two are going to spend the rest of their lives together. But not here."

"We can blame this all on Lydeck. I'm sure he manipulated Ki-ok into doing his dirty work. Lydeck is smarter than I gave him credit for, more than a little misguided, but smart. He eliminated my allies and took control of the Council. And if I do anything to stop him…well, I can't. He's now Commander of the colony. Or will be, once the Council reopens." Nok squatted next to Keerka.

"Nok, did you hear what I said? I'm trying to tell you something." Keerka leaned in against him, making sure she had his attention. "Our son will have to leave as soon as he and Kicki get their first molt."

Nok's body tensed. "What? Why in the name of the Ancients would he have to leave?"

"It's Kicki," Keerka said in a calm voice. "She has to go, and Leeg has to be with her."

Nok wanted to stand and walk out his frustration, but the weight of Keerka's body pressed against him kept him in place. "All right; what's going on with Kicki?"

"First let me say that I spoke with Packt this morning. And yes, I know what has happened to her since then. Packt told me that Kicki is an Oracle.

I'm not sure what that means or how it works. But the thing is, she can see events in the distant future and sometimes just before they happen."

"An Oracle?" Like many penguins, Nok had heard the stories. "All right; it's a little hard to comprehend, but all right, Kicki's an Oracle. What does that have to do with our son?"

Keerka leaned back from Nok. "If the Royal Emperors find out about her or worse, if this penguin called Aperion finds her, we will all suffer and Kicki will die."

"Wait, wait, wait. Who is Aperion? And why would he want to kill Kicki?"

Keerka repeated everything that Packt had told her and told Nok about what she had witnessed with Kicki.

Nok shook his head repeatedly. "No, I can't let him go. I won't." He had felt tired before, but now he felt exhausted. Why couldn't the world leave him in peace and let him live a normal penguin's life? He stared at his mate, watching the faint outlines of her face in the darkness. Nok decided that it was time to swim a little faster. "Do you really believe all of this?"

"Yes. Kicki is what Packt said she is."

Nok let out a long and tired sigh. "Then I guess I'll have to let him find his place in the sea, won't I? Who knows; maybe he'll come back one day and meet all of his future brothers and sisters."

Keerka coughed a laugh and stood. "Let's just see where the tide carries us and we'll go from there."

"Wait. Are you all right to stand?" Nok said, standing close for her to lean on him.

"Do you really want to sit here and wait for news about our son? Or do you want to find out for yourself?"

"Can you make it that far? What if we have to fight our way to him?"

Keerka snorted. "I know a short-cut, and I think I'll let you handle the fighting for now…maybe. Actually, I kind of doubt that."

CHAPTER 41

Lydeck walked through the corridors of the warrens like a little emperor. Now he would rid the colony of any malcontents and bring the colony under complete control. Soon Nok's son would be dead and the former commander would have nothing to fight for. Nok would endure Keerka's death, and then he would crumble, pleading for his own death. And Lydeck would oblige him.

"Lydeck, sir," a voice called from behind him. "Please wait, sir."

Bring on the sycophants, he thought at first but, then he recognized the voice and trembled in his hatred for Nok. "What is it, Tearsk? I thought I told you that I have no need for an apprentice." He put on his best air of civility for the commoners watching from the shadows.

"Yes, sir. That you did. But I was thinking. Now that you're Commander, you could use an assistant. I have a lot to learn, having been expelled from the apprentice program Nok put in place and all."

Lydeck leaned in close to Tearsk, his voice just above a whisper. "Thinking is not your strength, fledgling. Leave it to those who are capable of it."

"Yes, sir," Tearsk replied with the same amount of enthusiasm. "But I'm sure you see that I am not a fledgling. I may be young, but I'm not as incapable as you have suggested."

"Go away, Tearsk, I'm busy." Lydeck turned to leave, but Tearsk jumped in front of him. "Step aside. Being disrespectful to the Commander of the Council of Order has its own set of repercussions."

"I'm not being disrespectful, sir. I am merely trying to make you see that I'm not as stupid as you think I am," Tearsk said, blocking Lydeck's path once again.

"I will admit that your manner of speaking has improved since I last saw you, but I know plenty of penguins who speak just as well as you. Just like you, they have the intelligence of kelp. Now step aside." He pushed his way past him instead of slapping him away.

Again, Tearsk ran in front of him. "Even kelp has a purpose, sir. Without kelp, what would we have to hunt? The creatures that live in the kelp are our food. I'm sure that by me being your appointed apprentice you could teach me something. At least, you're supposed to. It was Commander Nok's order."

Lydeck stopped trying to get around the persistent Rockhopper. "I am Commander now, and I will rescind his orders. Now for the last time, and I hope your simple mind can understand this, get out of my way or I will make you regret that your parents even hatched you. Do you understand?"

Tearsk stood beak to beak with Lydeck. He was every bit as tall as him, but he lacked the muscle structure of a mature male. For a moment it seemed like Tearsk didn't care. "Yes, I understand," he said and stepped out of Lydeck's way.

"Surprise, surprise, a clump of tusset grass can see reason," Lydeck said as he brushed Tearsk aside.

Tearsk watched Lydeck for moment as he walked away. "Is it true what they say, that the only reason you survived the poaching ship was because you pushed Kakerk and Teek in front of you when the men came for you? They died and you were bagged. That you're a sniveling, manipulative coward who has other Rockhoppers do the work you refuse to do? Please tell me that none of these things are true about our new Commander."

Lydeck rushed the young male and knocked him to the ground. "Who says these things? Speak now or take it with you to the Great Sea!"

"So you don't only kill old and weak females and fledglings, you kill adolescent Rockhoppers as well?" Tearsk looked around, spotted a spectator. "Did you hear our new Commander threaten my life?" The onlooker ducked back into his alcove when he saw that he had been spotted.

Lydeck looked around and realized the spectacle he was making. He hopped on Tearsk's chest and leaned his head down until his beak rested against his ear. "Maybe you are cleverer than I thought, or maybe you're just too stupid to know when to shut up. But know this, I will make you pay. I will make your father pay and I will make your mother pay. You will watch them die before I see that you join them. I suggest to you that you don't follow me, or else my patience might run out." He hopped off the youth and continued his trek down the passage.

Tearsk stood up to watch him leave. "Will my grandfather pay too? How about my Aunt Kuskous?"

Lydeck hesitated and considered making an example of disobedience right then, but he thought better of it and kept walking.

CHAPTER 42

Still fuming over Tearsk and his insolence, Lydeck rushed toward the military quarters. He had fallen behind schedule and he had to get to Sergeant Kuk-kek and ensure his loyalty. Ki-ok couldn't demand loyalty the way Kairg could, and he had no doubts that the colonel would hold allegiance to Nok, even if it meant stripping him of his rank or banishment. He entered the quarters to find Kuk-kek talking to Sergeant Trarck. Panic set in. He couldn't hold power if those under Ki-ok's command, and by proxy under Kuk-kek, held loyalty to the opposition. The few Shadow Warriors wouldn't fare well against a force as strong-willed as the Rockhoppers.

Lydeck composed himself before he approached the pair. "Sergeant Trarck, so glad to see that you haven't given yourself over to lawlessness. I feared you might have felt that you owed fealty to Nok."

Trarck raised himself to his full height, standing a couple of inches taller than Lydeck. "I am under the command of Colonel Kairg, Lydeck. You obtained the title of Commander illegally and you will soon be brought to justice."

"That's Commander Lydeck to you, Sergeant." Lydeck looked between Kuk-kek and Trarck. "And whatever are these accusations? I guarantee you that I have done nothing illegal. You were there. I am the legally elected Commander of the Council. If you have proof otherwise, I suggest you present it to me; otherwise, keep your accusations to yourself. And while we are speaking of illegal activities, if Colonel Kairg has pledged loyalty to any entity other than the Council of Order and the Ministry of Defense, both of which are under my command, then he will be considered an outlaw and a traitor, and he will be tried as such."

"Committing murder to obtain the vote is a crime punishable by death. I guarantee you that your actions will be brought to light and you will be executed for your acts." Trarck turned his attention back to Kuk-kek.

"Again Sergeant, if you have any evidence that I had anything to do with what I can only assume is the unfortunate death of our dear old Packt, then tell me now." Lydeck met Trarck's eyes and waited for a response. "I thought not, Sergeant. I can tell by your actions here that you are in league with Nok and Colonel Kairg and that they may be planning a coup. Or perhaps it is you who is planning an uprising. After all, you were nominated for Commander as well and you were defeated."

Trarck turned away and faced Kuk-kek once again. "You know what I've told you is the truth, Sergeant. The choice is yours. Don't make a decision that you'll regret."

Kuk-kek looked at Lydeck and back to Trarck. "I'm sorry, Sergeant. Lydeck is now the legally elected Commander, and I am subject to the laws and edicts of the Ministry. In fact we both are. It is not up to us to choose when we follow the laws."

"Very good, Sergeant Kuk-kek. It appears that you are in line for a promotion. How does General sound to you?" Lydeck said.

"When the lawmakers have broken the laws to get here, then we do have the choice, Kuk-kek," Trarck said as he climbed a low rock. He stood high and surveyed the view of hundreds of yellow crests floating on a sea of black. He looked back at Lydeck who narrowed his eyes. "Fellow Rockhoppers, Lydeck has obtained the position of Commander through venal and felonious means. I am under orders given to me by Colonel Kairg to bring you with me into the lowest reaches of the warren where we will find that Lydeck has allied with the Royal Emperors. More specifically, Shadow Warriors. If you feel that Lydeck's actions are not in the best interest of the colony, then follow me." He hopped from the rock and began to run.

"What are you doing?" Lydeck shouted at Kuk-kek. "Stop him. Arrest him! He is inciting rebellion."

When Kuk-kek hesitated, Lydeck leapt on to the rock. "You will stop this instant. I am the lawful Commander of the Colony. I have been legally and rightfully elected. If you choose to follow Sergeant Trarck, then you'll be charged with treason." When half of the multitude stopped their exodus, he hopped back down and approached Kuk-kek with fire burning in his eyes.

Kuk-kek faced Commander Lydeck with his head bowed. "I apologize, Commander. But these are Rockhoppers we have known our whole lives. We have fought alongside of them and we have been raised alongside of them. Is there not a better way?"

"They are traitors, Sergeant. And they are criminals and should be treated as such. Their actions jeopardize the safety and wellbeing of our entire colony. Now, will you fulfill your duties and protect our colony from all threats, or would you like to be considered a traitor to the colony as well?" Lydeck braced himself for another defection. With a large portion of the Defense Ministry forces following Trarck out of the cavernous space, he could ill-afford losing another soldier.

Kuk-kek straightened and lifted his beak. "No, sir. I will uphold the laws and protect our colony as directed."

"Very good, Sergeant. You just might yet get that promotion. Now take sergeant Trarck into custody. Quickly, before this gets completely out of control." Lydeck watched Kuk-kek disappear into the crowd.

CHAPTER 43

Kicki nudged Tearsk into an antechamber and the two watched as hundreds of Rockhoppers rushed by with Sergeant Trarck in the lead. They could hear the squawking of brawls breaking out near the rear of the procession as Kuk-kek's forces attempted to stop the defectors.

Tearsk paced nervously in the darkness. "I don't think I did a very good job of delaying Lydeck. It sounds like Sergeant Trarck didn't get all of the warriors to go with him."

"You did great. If you hadn't done what you did, they would all be under Lydeck's command." Kicki edged to the opening for a better look and was nearly knocked to the ground as two scuffling Rockhoppers hit the wall beside her. She watched as one Rockhopper kicked the other back and ran to join Sergeant Trarck's group. "This could have been a lot worse."

"I know it could have been—I thought Lydeck was going to kill me. He said he will, too." Tearsk walked to the furthest wall and lurched. "You must think I'm the biggest coward, me getting sick because of this."

Kicki came to his side and used her best motherly voice. "Not at all. What you did was very brave. You confronted the enemy. Lydeck is very dangerous."

Kicki felt a pang of guilt. She had put Tearsk in harm's way without knowing the outcome. It was one thing to risk combat veterans; they had the experience to handle dangerous situations, and she could see the positive outcomes outweighed the negative. Tearsk was barely a year older than her and she couldn't see his fate. Try as she may, she still couldn't get any more than the vaguest impressions about Tearsk.

She tried to concentrate; the possibilities still swam in the shadows around her but in ever decreasing numbers. Her work had accomplished something. Without warning, the dark cavern swirled, the images mingled with the spinning rock until they became a blur of speed. She closed her eyes but the images kept spinning. All she could see were the streaks of gray and black and yellow. The spinning stopped as suddenly as it began.

She cautiously opened her eyes and saw a shoreline below her. She floated above like a pin feather caught on the wind. She drifted down toward the black sand beach. What she saw didn't seem right. She had only seen the black beaches of her home twice, and this didn't look like what she had seen. The beach appeared to be undulating, as if the waves were below the sand pushing it up and letting it fall. Her minds eye moved closer and she saw that it was not sand at all, but mounds of black and white. She tried to pull back, not wanting to see what she already knew she would see.

At last, she stood on what was not sand but the corpses of thousands of dead penguins, washed up on a foreign shore as far as she could see. The Seeing came in flashes, and every image showed the same as the first; millions of penguins on hundreds of shores. The scavengers taking their first tentative bites on the bounty of a sudden and mass extinction. Kicki opened her eyes and returned to the present with a scream.

Tearsk fell backwards. "Kicki, are you all right? What happened?" he said, getting back to his feet.

Kicki couldn't say a word. She trembled, lying on the ground, not quite aware of her surroundings.

"Kicki," Tearsk said slowly. "Are you all right?"

She stood and planted her feet firmly on the rocky ground, trying to rid herself of the sensation of standing on the dead. Tearsk called to her once more and she finally heard his voice. "No, I'm not all right. I never will be all right again."

"What do you mean? What happened? One moment you were talking to me and the next you were spinning until you fell down."

"None of this really matters. What happens here, the fighting, the Rockhoppers, the Royals, Lydeck; we're all dead. This will all come to an end."

"You're scaring me, Kicki. It's my job to scare you. Not the other way around." Tearsk took a cautious step closer to her. "Look at me, Kicki."

She looked up at him with eyes still wide from shock. "I saw it. I saw the end of our kind. It will happen soon. How soon, I don't know. But it will happen."

Tearsk swallowed hard. "How could you see something that's not real?"

"I can see things, Tearsk. That's how I knew to send you to delay Lydeck. I've been playing with the future. I don't understand it, so don't ask me to explain. I knew what Lydeck would do if he beat Trarck to the military. I knew Ki-ok would take Leeg. All day it's been coming to me, slow at first and now, it's too fast for me to follow. I don't understand how or why things are happening. I only know that I can change what might happen. I'm not old enough for this, Tearsk. I don't want to be an Oracle. I just want to… " Her body quivered and she saw Leeg. The Shadow Warriors stood over him. She stumbled back. "It's Leeg. I don't think the others will get to him in time. Go, Tearsk. He's in the cave. The Shadow Warriors will kill him. Run!"

Tearsk hesitated. "If this is some prank to get back at me—"

"It's not. I swear to you, it's not. Just go. Hurry. You won't be able to fight them—you just have to delay them."

Tearsk waited another second. "I'm good at delaying penguins," he said and ran out of the chamber.

Kicki leaned against the wall. The Seeing had slowed down, giving her a chance to breathe. She thought about going to help, but her legs gave out.

She could do no more. The events would unfold as they must. She fell to her stomach and her eyes grew heavy as the images continued their dance.

CHAPTER 44

Tretak pushed her way through the crowd of Rockhoppers and found Lydeck standing at the head, delivering a useless speech about his magnificence. He had found two Rockhoppers sycophantic enough to be lured into act as bodyguards. She was glad to see that Kuk-kek had not volunteered for the position. His dedication to duty was unsurpassed in the ranks of the ministry and she could hold no blame against him following the edicts of the ministry. And he was one of the very few Rockhoppers who she even marginally considered a friend. Be that as it may, he would be a formidable opponent if it came to it and she had no desire for this to come to a fight.

Tretak stood before the new Commander waiting for him to turn his pontifical gaze upon her. His arrogance seemed to be growing by the minute. "Commander Lydeck," she said with exaggerated patience. "I need to speak with you immediately." The pair of guards stepped in front of Lydeck and Tretak nearly burst into a laugh. He was either putting on a show of elitism or he was actually very scared that someone would attempt to drive a beak between his wings.

"No, no, she is fine," Lydeck said, waving the guards away. "What do we need to speak about?"

"I think it would best if we went someplace a little more private."

"Why Tretak, I haven't the time at the moment to steal away with you alone, but I thank you for the offer," Lydeck said, raising his voice so that those around them could hear.

"Lieutenant Ki-ok needs your help. They are after him and they'll kill him." She spoke loud enough for those nearby to hear.

Any mirth, no matter how false, that was in Lydeck's eyes disappeared. He stepped close to Tretak. "Ki-ok's fate is of little concern to me now. His usefulness has expired. Better that he remain silent."

"He will tell Kairg. And there will be an investigation. The Tribunal—"

"The Tribunal will no longer exist. As soon as I shore up my authority and be rid of the traitors, I will see that my allies *disband* the Tribunal. I will be the law, I will control the Ministry."

"So you mean not to help Ki-ok? Without him, you would never have become Commander."

"And without him I will be able to keep it that way." Lydeck turned his back on her.

She had to think of something quick while Ki-ok was still alive. She had no doubts that once he was found they would kill him on the spot. She watched his pompous stride as he walked back to the protection of his guards. And then it hit her like an icy South Atlantic wave. *Shore up your authority, huh?* She looked at Kuk-kek, who had been curiously watching their conversation. "You mean to tell me that you intend to ignore Lieutenant Ki-ok's pleas for help? By the Ancients, you are the Commander of the Colony. All you have to do is go there and put a stop to this."

Tretak watched with a glint of satisfaction as Lydeck's torso began to rapidly rise and fall with each angry breath. He spun around and tried to force his composure. She stepped back just in case the coward actually mustered the courage to do something rash. He gave her a look that told her that her usefulness was over as well.

Lydeck's expression changed to a forced calm. "Council member Tretak, surely you don't expect me to rush into a situation that could get me killed for his sake. I am the Commander; I have to use caution."

"Did Nok use caution when you were being held on the human ship? No, he went into a situation that could have easily gotten him killed and saved your life. Ki-ok is your friend. You have to help him." Tretak noticed that a crowd of Rockhopper warriors had gathered around.

Lydeck's eyes shifted, seeming to gauge the mood of the crowd. "Ki-ok is far from being a friend. And I believe he had some trouble at the Falklands, didn't he? I can find a Rockhopper better suited to lead my forces. While I understand the gravity of the lieutenant's predicament, there is little I can do."

"That's not true. Ki-ok told me that you were a friend, someone he could trust," Kuk-kek interjected. "As far as having trouble at the Falkland campaign, at least he was there."

Tretak could see Lydeck attempting to keep his anger under control. Time to push him a little further. "You have an army right here before you. Are you going to lead them down there and save Ki-ok and possibly put an end to the rebellion before it gains more momentum? Because I won't stand for it…a Rockhopper dying unaided and alone."

Lydeck seethed and tapped his flipper against his side nervously. "Very well, Tretak. Sergeant Kuk-kek, rouse the forces; we are going to save Ki-ok." As Kuk-kek went to see about his duties Lydeck approached Tretak. "I don't know what you're up to, but I assure you, that when this is over, you will be punished."

"I'm sorry, Commander. I only want what's best for every member of the colony." She paused until a few penguins pushed by. "You will help Ki-ok. If it weren't for him, you'd still be sitting as a mere Council member while Trarck became Commander."

"That may be true, but as you well know, Ki-ok is a liability." Lydeck waited until more Rockhoppers passed, "just as you have become. I'm sure my allies will agree. All of this to protect your friend."

Tretak faced Lydeck beak to beak. "I don't have friends." The two locked eyes. Neither backed down, but Tretak caught an unmistakable glint of fear in Lydeck's eyes. Her own eyes narrowed in satisfaction.

"Sir, the troops are in order," Kuk-kek said, breaking the stare down.

Lydeck's eyes shifted between Kuk-kek and Tretak. "Very well, Sergeant."

"Time to get your feet wet, Commander," Tretak said as Lydeck pushed his guards forward.

CHAPTER 45

Tearsk ran. He wanted nothing more than to stop, but he couldn't stop. He had to save Leeg. If he saved Leeg, he could actually be a hero and past transgressions might be forgiven and forgotten. But he had to keep running.

Tearsk had spent enough time in the lower reaches of the warrens to know his way around pretty well. He knew the alternate routes that not even the eldest member of the colony knew about. He also knew the shortest path was the darkest. He heard the stragglers of Trarck's warriors ahead of him. He hopped onto another rock, slowed his pace and crept behind them, keeping his distance and hiding in the crags.

The procession's pace was excruciatingly slow, and it was all Tearsk could do to keep from shouting and tell them to speed along. Leeg's life was on the line, after all. He ducked into another crag and waited again. He considered just pushing his way through the crowd until he realized he was almost to the shortcut. The entrance looked like nothing more than a fissure in the rock. When the last of the warriors passed the crevice, he rushed forward and squeezed his way in. After scraping his way along for a couple of meters, the gap opened to a wider path. He walked a little faster but not too fast. He knew from painful experience that the cavern was littered with small stalactites and stalagmites. Taking one cautious step after another and feeling each footfall before he stepped, he soon realized that the shortcut in this situation was anything but.

Tearsk knew that each moment he was delayed was a moment closer to Leeg dying. He had to make a choice: either go back the way he had come or throw caution to the wind and hope he didn't trip and impale himself. "This way is quicker," he said to convince himself. He paused after he spoke. Something in the reverberation of his voice made him stop and listen. He could hear the steady dripping of water splashing into a small unseen pool, the hushed babble of water flowing further into the abyss, and the faint sound of something scratching against rock.

Tearsk crept forward, trying to remain silent. He listened, straining his ears to hear what he had heard before. Nothing. "I'm wasting time." He firmed his beak and started walking as fast he safely could. If he remembered the path correctly, he would soon be able to see a hint of light which would signal his exit and put him near the cave. He picked up his pace a little more, protruding his stomach so that he could feel any obstacle before he tripped over it. He couldn't help but yelp when the top of his head scraped the bottom of a stalactite.

He stood for a moment until the first pulsations of throbbing pain came to an end. He heard a noise again, followed by another more distinct scuffling. Tearsk couldn't wait any longer. He hoped whatever was hiding in the dark stayed hidden for a little longer. "Whatever you are, don't try to stop me, because you'll regret it."

"Tearsk?" a voice called out.

"Who's there?" He felt his way closer to the sounds.

"It's Nok and Keerka," Nok said.

"Commander Nok, what are you doing down here?" He rushed forward and bumped into Keerka.

"Careful," Keerka warned.

"We were on our way to help find Leeg, but Keerka's hurt and had to stop. What are you doing here?"

"Kicki sent me. I'm going to get Leeg. Don't you worry, I'll get him."

"Kicki?" said Keerka. "What did she say?"

"She said that Kairg and Trarck won't get there in time. Now if you don't mind, I have to go save your son." He pushed off through the darkness, bumping into dripstones and reciting the words he had overheard the adults say which weren't supposed to be said in polite company. He ignored the calls of Nok and Keerka urging him to stop, that it was too dangerous and foolish to confront Ki-ok and Shadow Warriors. It was his chance to prove his character, to prove his worth. Nothing was going to stop him.

Tearsk saw the faint glow of the exit ahead but at the bottom of a steep slope. The light was dim, but it seemed like a full moon, guiding him to his destiny. The only problem being the slope was slippery and somewhat treacherous. There was another way, but he hated being delayed any further. He took a deep breath, found his footing and hesitated. He knew the dripstones were practically nonexistent on the incline, but his experience in spelunking was such that he really had no idea what to expect. He let out a breath and scooted down until his foot found a perch. He repeated the process and found the next purchase. Feeling better about what he was doing, Tearsk scooted forward, his foot found a rock which promptly gave way. He did his best not to shout as he went sliding through the darkness at an alarming speed.

He continued his downward spin—he was going break his legs at the bottom, he would get wedged in the crevasse, where he would starve to death and his bloated corpse would block the exit; Leeg would die as well because of his failure. In a hundred generations some Rockhopper would find what was left of his bones and wonder how stupid a Rockhopper had to be to die in a rock. He hit the bottom with an agonizing *whump* and realized none of his predictions would come true. He hurt, but nothing had broken.

Tearsk squeezed through the crevice, and entered the cave he had so often teased the fledglings and chicks about. The cave was bright by comparison and smelled of fresh seawater. The breaths and gasps of the waves breaking just below the breach made him feel like he was in the stomach of a whale. He stealthily stumbled over a rock and rolled behind another to keep out of sight. He heard voices across the pool and lifted his head for a peek.

He could make out the forms of Colonel Kairg, Cleyed and Cosk; beyond that, he could see a form which had to belong to Ki-ok and next to him, a tiny lump, which was Leeg. His heart skipped a beat, thinking he had gotten there too late, but then he clearly heard Kairg telling Leeg that it would be all right. Maybe Kicki had been wrong. Colonel Kairg could handle this. His gaze drifted up toward the large gap in the cliff wall and he felt a chill crawl up his spine. Standing, silhouetted by the waning daylight, he saw the forms of at least four Shadow Warriors. No, the colonel would need unexpected help.

Tearsk scurried and hid behind a column formed by conjoined dripstones. He went to the pool and carefully paddled across without making the slightest splash. He climbed the bank and squeezed into a nook just below Colonel Kairg. He listened to the demands and threats the Colonel issued to Ki-ok and waited. He needed a break, an opportunity to act without risking Leeg's life or his own. While he sat and waited, he realized that there would be no way to rescue Leeg without risking his own life. "But that's what heroes do, right?" he said in a tiny whisper.

CHAPTER 46

"Ki-ok, let him go. You can't win, you can't escape, and if you let him go, there's a chance you might get away with only being banished and receiving the stigma." Colonel Kairg took a careful step forward and Ki-ok made a motion as if he would peck Leeg. Kairg backed off and eyed the Shadow Warriors entering the breach. They were huge, bigger than he remembered.

"The stigma? Is that all, Colonel? Is that all? You pluck my crest and send me to the sea alone? That's just a prolonged death sentence and you know that. You know that, Colonel." Ki-ok paced relentlessly, taking small steps and knocking Leeg back every time it looked as if he mustered enough gumption to make an escape. "Lydeck promised me the position of War Chief. He is the Commander now, not Nok, and you certainly will not hold power over me for long. Not long at all."

Kairg looked at Cosk and Cleyed for suggestions. They needed proof that Lydeck had ordered the murder of Packt and Ki-ok was the only who could give them that proof. "There is no such position as War Chief, Ki-ok, you know this. He lied, he used you. And where is he now? He set you up to take the fall while he took the position and power of Commander. And do you think your Royal Emperor friends up there give a seal's tail about you? Lydeck will probably have you killed, just like he had you kill Packt."

"He'll create the position of War Chief, and if he tries to kill me, he'll find that it is not so easy. Not easy at all." He spotted Leeg get up and attempt to run and slapped him down. "Stay down."

Cleyed stepped in. "Are you really so stupid, Ki-ok? Lydeck would never do anybody such favors. Look what he's done. He has become allies with our enemies. More Royals will come and we will be subjugated to them. It's time for this foolishness to end. Now let Leeg go and be done with this."

The Shadow Warriors stepped closer. "Finish the task," one said to the would-be War Chief.

Ki-ok looked at the Shadow Warriors and back to Kairg. "It's too late for that now. Once I kill Leeg, Nok will no longer be a factor. He will see just what his policies and arrogance has cost him and he will simply disappear. Disappear. Now go away unless you want to watch what will happen."

Kairg had to stall him. "I'm not going anywhere, Ki-ok. You are a coward now, you have always been a coward, and you always will be a coward. I doubt that you have the courage to do it. This is your last chance to give the child up and surrender."

"You seem to be under the impression that I am the same Rockhopper you have berated for a year now," grumbled Ki-ok. "You will find I am quite formidable."

"Killing old females and fledglings does not make you formidable. It only proves that you are a pathetic coward." Kairg caught a wisp of motion to his left and casually glanced over, hoping Trarck had arrived. He was surprised to see that it wasn't Trarck or any other warrior, but a young adult whom he recognized but couldn't put a name to. He kept his eyes forward, but kept the motion in his peripheral. Whoever it was, he or she was up to something. "I've had enough of this, Ki-ok. Let him go, or I will save you the trouble of facing the Tribunal and kill you where you stand."

Ki-ok started to speak, but a blur of motion caught his eye. A young Rockhopper, so young that his plume had only just begun to sprout, dashed up the large sloping rock and headed straight toward him. The entire group stood dumbfounded. They watched Tearsk run directly toward Leeg's captor. When Colonel Kairg saw what the youth was about to do, he took a couple of steps toward Ki-ok.

The next instant, Tearsk leapt with claws forward and impacted solidly with Ki-ok. Ki-ok tumbled over and Tearsk flopped to his back. The youth was to his feet in a flash. Ki-ok struggled to right himself, but Tearsk hopped on his chest and inflicted several savage pecks before he pushed Leeg toward Kairg and darted away.

Colonel Kairg took Leeg and ushered him toward Cleyed and Cosk. He turned back toward Ki-ok, fully intent on killing him right then, but the Shadow Warriors were on the move. He turned tail and ran, joining the others as they splashed across the pool. The group shuffled out of the water and spotted Tearsk trying to get to his feet, Lydeck standing over him. Kairg reacted immediately. "Stay away from him, Lydeck."

Lydeck looked up and stepped toward Kairg in his most haughty manner. "Colonel Kairg, what an unexpected and unpleasant surprise to find you here. Ah, and Council members Cleyed and Cosk. Up to something treasonous, no doubt? Sergeant Kuk-kek, arrest them and bring the fledgling to me."

Kairg stepped in front of Leeg. "Don't even try it, Kuk-kek. I am still your commanding officer. You had better consider your loyalties."

Kuk-kek looked back to Lydeck. Lydeck rolled his head, acting as if it were a bother. "Ah, yes, that commanding officer issue. I have to rectify that at once. Colonel Kairg, as Commander of the Colony, I proclaim that you are officially relieved of duty. Now you may arrest them, Sergeant. Carry out your orders."

The ruckus calls of hundreds of Rockhoppers interrupted the standoff as Rockhoppers from both factions began squawking at one another from outside of the cave—neither side wanting to fight, but neither willing to back down. Kairg took the opportunity and spoke to Kuk-kek. "Look at who your commander has allied himself with. The Royals are our enemy. They have killed Rockhoppers. And before long, the Royals will have control of our colony. Is that what you want?"

Lydeck's bodyguards burst in, followed by Sergeant Trarck and Tretak. The guards took up position next to Lydeck, who scowled at them. "Tretak, I have done as requested. I have come here to rescue Ki-ok, but as you see, he is nowhere in sight."

Kairg spun around and saw for himself that Ki-ok was indeed gone. He also took notice that six Shadow Warriors were standing in the pool just behind them. As he watched them, he spotted a bubble percolating up in the pool just to the right of them. At least he knew where Ki-ok was now. But that wouldn't matter if he didn't get away from the Royals creeping up behind him. He urged his comrades forward and Sergeant Trarck joined him. "Call off your brutes, Lydeck."

The shouting outside of the cave became louder as the opposing forces began shoving one another. Several Rockhoppers spilled into the cave. "Sergeant Kuk-kek, do get control over your soldiers."

"These are not under my command, Commander," Kuk-kek said as he stepped next to Kairg.

"Am I to understand that you have gone the way of traitor as well, Sergeant Kuk-kek?" Lydeck backed slowly away, trying to place his guards between him and Kairg and the others.

"If you have made an alliance with these monsters, then it's you who are the traitor."

Another noise from behind Lydeck caught everyone's attention as Nok and Keerka exited the crevice Tearsk had come through.

"What? Is the entire colony coming down here?" Lydeck said as he stepped toward the Shadow Warriors. His body guards spotted the Shadows, exchanged worried looks and fled, leaving Lydeck exposed and alone. He watched them leave with obvious disgust and frustration.

"Commander Nok, Keerka," Kairg said. He stepped aside and nudged

Leeg toward his parents. Ignoring the happy reunion, Kairg turned back toward Lydeck. The Shadows were no longer at his back, but that still didn't make him feel any safer. "Lydeck, your time is done here. You will be brought before the Tribunal and charged with the murders of Packt, Eeco and kidnapping with intent to murder Leeg."

Lydeck laughed. "What proof do you have of this, Colonel?"

Kairg looked at Tretak. "I'm the proof. Me and Lieutenant Ki-ok."

Ki-ok emerged from the pool and looked warily at Colonel Kairg and Nok. He surveyed the situation and shook the water from his dense feathers. "Lydeck did not kill Packt or Eeco. It was me. It was me." He looked at Lydeck who was giving him an unmistakable look of warning. "But it was Lydeck who asked me to do these things. He promised me a position of power and the opportunity to be seen as the hero of the colony, not the coward you see standing before you."

"Lies," Lydeck blurted out. "Again, what proof do you have? He is obviously attempting to push the blame from him to someone else. I assure you that the lieutenant acted on his own fruition. You have your murderer; now, let's take him to the Tribunal and be done with this nonsense."

"They aren't lies," Tretak said. "I was there. I heard him and I saw him." She stared at Lydeck, her eyes burning with hatred.

Colonel Kairg stepped forward. He looked at Ki-ok. He had been exceptionally hard on him since the battle at the Falklands. He blamed him for his mate's death there. The lieutenant's failure to attack had made him an easy target of guilt. But now Kairg took some of the blame for himself. Had he not been so hard on Ki-ok, would he have still resorted to murder to get respect and approval? Regardless, it was Ki-ok who had committed the crimes and Lydeck who influenced him. "Commander Lydeck, you are under arrest for treason and murder. Surrender yourself now."

Lydeck scoffed. He looked to the Shadow Warriors. "Well, don't just stand there, kill them. Kill them all!"

CHAPTER 47

Tretak heard both Sergeant Kuk-kek and Trarck call their troops to battle and took advantage of the chaos to pursue her quarry. She ducked under the wild stab of a Shadow and spotted him edging back toward the pool. "No, you're not getting away that easily." She rushed toward Lydeck who spotted her and ran along the water. She dove into the pool and swam along the edge until she caught up to him. She sprung from the water, knocking Lydeck down to the ground.

Lydeck stood and lashed out with his beak, narrowly missing her face. He fled once again, diving into the pool to make his escape.

Tretak dove in behind him and latched onto his foot with her beak. Lydeck tried to shake her loose, but she held tight, hoping to inflict as much damage as possible while preventing him from escaping. He flailed to the surface, which gave her the room to twist her body while still holding his foot. She felt the snap of a breaking toe, and Lydeck thrashed harder until she finally lost her grip.

Lydeck scrambled out of the water and tried to limp away, but Tretak was right behind him. She stabbed at his back, and moved in for the kill as he tried to stand. She leapt, slamming her body into his. Lydeck squirmed away. Tretak got her feet and pounced, this time keeping him pinned to the ground. She slashed at his chest. Lydeck chirped and she came down on him again. He let out an even more pitiable bleat.

"Why? Why did you betray me?" Lydeck asked, almost pleading. "You would have become the most powerful female Rockhopper the colony had ever known. You could have had it all."

"Have it all? Have what, exactly?" Tretak spat. She couldn't believe how delusional he actually was. She jabbed her beak into his chest once more. "I did have all I ever wanted. Now…now there's just life and revenge. Look me in the eye, Lydeck. Now think back, many tides ago. It was a day like any other day. Any other day, that is, until the humans came."

"The humans came on many days. How am I—"

She slapped him again. "Shut up. The warrens were full, and some of us had to nest close to the shore. Except for you; no sane female would ever take you as a mate. We ran from them, we climbed. I made it up the rocks. I looked back to my mate and I saw you struggling to climb. The humans were getting closer, their pouches and clubs in hand, catching Rockhoppers in their sacks and beating them with their weapons. You were as good as caught when my mate boosted you up. You made it. But instead of running, you laid there like a helpless chick. My mate had nearly scaled the rock, but the humans were right behind him. And how did you repay his help?"

Lydeck looked at Tretak, his eyes narrow from pain.

"That's right. You kicked him down right into their filthy hands. And *then* you ran like the worthless coward you have always been."

"I panicked. I swear, it wasn't intentional. They were right on us. What was I to do?"

"Shut up." She slashed at his face with her beak. "Just killing you wasn't enough. I wanted them all to see just what a scheming, useless, pathetic penguin you are. You thought you could just take over the Council and we would all bow to your rule. Now you have nothing. The entire colony sees you for who you are and they hate you. And now you're going to die with nothing."

Lydeck's eyes shifted back and forth, finally resting on Tretak. "I'm guilty, it's true. But before you kill me, let me say one last thing."

"And what is that?"

His eyes narrowed. "Always watch your back."

"What?" Her confusion ended when her head met the slap of a Shadow Warrior's flipper. She smacked against a rock and slid to the ground. Lying on her back with her consciousness fading, the last thing she heard was Lydeck telling the Shadow Warrior to kill her.

CHAPTER 48

Sergeant Trarck pushed his way to the front of the line along with Nok, Colonel Kairg, Sergeant Kuk-kek, and Cleyed. Six Rockhoppers had already fallen to the Shadow Warriors. "I hate Royal Emperors."

"I couldn't agree more, Sergeant," Kairg said. "Commander Nok, is your son safe?"

"Yes, Colonel, he is. Keerka has him and is taking him to our chambers. And thank you again," Nok said without taking his eyes off of the line of Shadow Warriors.

"It's Tearsk you should be thanking. He saved him, not me."

"You can thank me later," Tearsk said, coming to Nok's side.

Trarck looked at the young Rockhopper. "You probably shouldn't be here. These things aren't like any penguins you've ever known."

Kairg looked at Tearsk from the corner of his eye. "Tearsk is as brave as any penguin here. I'll be proud to have him fight at our side."

Nok agreed. "Stick to the plan—we stay together and take them out one at a time."

Without another word, five of the bravest fighters in the colony rushed the lead Shadow Warrior. The Shadow spread its wings, lowered its head with beak forward and let out a horrifying screech. The attack group, undaunted by the display, slammed into the Royal with enough force to knock it back a few steps. Nok and Cleyed pressed forward and stabbed at its lower body. Trarck piggy-backed off of Kairg and hit it in the face with his feet. Kuk-kek dove behind the Shadow's legs, and the force of the other's push sent it falling to its back.

Sergeant Trarck pounced on the Shadow Warrior's chest and tore into its throat. He raised his head with blood and flesh falling from his beak. "Next," he said and the group followed his lead.

The next Shadow was preoccupied with a small band of Rockhoppers when Trarck bodily crashed into its side. The Shadow stumbled but kept its footing. It turned and wildly swung its flipper across, striking Trarck to the ground. It lowered its head to deal a lethal stab, but Tearsk struck it. The Warrior whipped its head back and looked at Tearsk. "That was very foolish," the Shadow said. "Now you will—"

Nok dug his beak into the Shadow Warrior's soft neck flesh and twisted. The Shadow raised its head, trying to fling Nok off. But Nok had done this kind of work before and clung tightly. The momentum of the swing tore the Shadow's flesh away. It howled in pain and rage as the Rockhoppers brought it down.

Nok had landed in the pool and came racing back into the fray.

"Nice one, Commander," Kairg said. "Are you all right, Sergeant?"

Trarck nodded, looking at Tearsk. He stood and surveyed the battle. Two of the Shadow Warriors fought back to back, stabbing and slashing at each attacker. "Shall we move to the next?"

"Lead the way," Kuk-kek said as he came beside him.

Trarck started to move but stopped. "Tretak," he blurted out and rushed away, ignoring the other's calls.

The Shadow Warrior stood over Tretak sizing up his victim. Trarck rushed in, howling, and hit the Shadow with all of his weight. It stumbled sideways. He pressed his advantage and attacked again, but the Shadow had braced for this attack and slapped Sergeant Trarck back. Trarck spotted Lydeck struggling to scurry up the other side of the pool, but the others would have to deal with him; he had bigger things to worry about at the moment. The Shadow lunged and stabbed at Trarck with its deadly beak, forcing him to retreat.

The Shadow Warrior continued to come at him. It attacked wildly while Trarck remained calm, easily evading the attacks. The Shadow reared back in frustration. Trarck saw the break he needed and charged forward, meeting the Shadow Warrior in its stomach and driving it back.

The Shadow Warrior back-stepped until it could no longer keep pace with the driving force of Sergeant Trarck. It fell to its back and Trarck fell with it, landing on the bigger penguin's chest. The two combatants locked eyes. The Shadow stabbed upward and caught Trarck in the shoulder. He howled in pain and rolled away from his assailant. He looked back and saw the Royal roll to its stomach and begin to stand. He spotted Nok and the others coming to his aid, but didn't wait for their help. He stood and hopped on the Shadow Warrior's back, knocking it back down. Trarck bit into the back of its neck, but the thick muscle and fat prevented any serious damage. He hopped off and circled to the top of its head. The Shadow looked at him and Trarck struck. He took out its left eye and spat it to the ground. And when the beast rolled, over writhing in pain he stabbed his beak into the other eye.

He stepped back and watched the Shadow Warrior screech and flail blindly on the ground. When he had enough of its screeching, he leapt on to its chest, tore into its neck, and silenced it immediately. He stood on top of his victim until its final twitch. When he hopped off he found Nok, Kairg, and the others staring at him with beaks agape.

"That was amazing," Tearsk blurted out.

"Where are the other two?" Trarck said.

"They fled across the pool," Nok said, still mesmerized by Trarck's display of brute force.

"After them," he said, stooping down to tend to Tretak. "Are you all right?"

Tretak glared at Trarck at first, but then softened. "Yes. I'm fine. Thanks."

She got to her feet and surveyed the cave.

Trarck nodded. He wanted to say more, but couldn't think of the words. He spotted Nok and the others rushing up the rocks on the other side of the pool. "I'm going after Lydeck," he said and left Tretak staring after him.

CHAPTER 49

Nok ran toward the breach and shouted at Lydeck. The other paid him no mind and joined the two remaining Shadow Warriors. Spray from the angry surf glistened on the black bodies as the last tendrils of daylight began to fade away. Neither side made a move to attack. A third penguin, a Royal Emperor, emerged from the gap and conversed with the Shadow Warriors.

Lydeck turned and faced the group of Rockhoppers. "This isn't over, Nok. My allies and I will return, and when we do you will find that we aren't so easily brushed aside."

The Royal Emperor leaned into Lydeck. "We won't be coming back. Mearna has decided on a different course of action, and she is no longer in need of this colony or island."

"Then it was...it was all for nothing. I did as you, no, as *she* asked. I took control of the Council. I gave you everything. What am I supposed to do now?"

"Do as you wish. You are welcome to air your grievances to Mearna. She might take pity on you—or she might not." The Shadow Warriors turned toward the opening.

Colonel Kairg, stepped forward. "We will hunt you down, Lydeck. I swear, I will make it my life's purpose to hunt you down and kill you."

Nok put his flipper up to stop him. "Let it go, Kairg. They have the advantage. He's injured—chances are, he won't even survive the surf."

Kairg huffed and looked at Lydeck. "As soon as you leave, we'll follow and catch you like the slimy squid you are."

Lydeck knew that would be something that the colonel would do. There was a reason they weren't attacking him; there had to be. He had to think of a lie to keep them off of his tail. "Do your best, Colonel. I would love for you to do just that. I was just informed that there is an entire battalion of Royal Emperors not more than a day out. Come chase me, Kairg. I would dearly love to see you end up as chum. And make no mistake. We will return and I will see you punished."

Tearsk padded over to him. "You go ahead Lydeck. You bring your allies. We'll know where and when you'll arrive, and we'll drive you back to the sea. We have an Oracle, and she'll be able to see what you have planned." Tearsk proudly turned back toward his comrades.

Lydeck looked at his Royal Emperor companions. All three knew the implications if this were true; though Lydeck's ideas were vastly different from the Royal's. He guessed that Tearsk had been instructed to delay him. If he had gotten to the troops sooner, this whole thing might have ended differently. Lydeck cheerfully turned away. The Shadow Warriors had already leapt into the surf. "Thank you, Tearsk. Your stupidity has been a great help. I'll be seeing you, Nok." He jumped feet first into the pounding waves and disappeared into the foam.

CHAPTER 50

Sergeant Kuk-kek approached Trarck, Nok and Colonel Kairg as they walked toward the main hall of the warrens. "Commander Nok, there was no sign of Lieutenant Ki-ok's body among the dead, sir. I've spoken with several witnesses, all of whom said he was last seen leaving the cave and headed back up. I am organizing search squads to track him down."

"Sir, if I may? I believe I know where I can find him," Sergeant Trarck said.

"Trarck, you know as well as I do that you'll be elected as Commander as soon as we open for the next Council meeting. So you don't need my permission to do anything."

Trarck cleared his throat. "Actually I was speaking to Colonel Kairg. He is the highest ranking officer at the moment."

"Oh...uh, yes, of course. That makes perfect sense. Sorry for the interruption," Nok said, quietly stepping back.

Trarck continued to stare at Kairg. "Colonel?"

"Huh? Yes. What he said." Kairg indicated Nok with his flipper. Trarck began to leave, but Kairg called him back. "Sergeant, wait for me. I would dearly love to be there when he is finally captured. Are you coming, Commander? I mean, Nok."

"I'll leave this work to the militia. I need to check in with Keerka and

Leeg and let them know I'm fine. Happy hunting," Nok said.

Nok listened to the others discuss their plans to capture Ki-ok as they walked away. For a moment, and only for a moment, he felt that familiar urge to join in the fight. But it passed as quickly as it came. He was finally out of the turmoil. He didn't harbor any delusions that he would never see combat again, he had a feeling that day would come sooner than he wanted, but at the very least, he no longer had the responsibility of putting another penguin's life on the line. He didn't have to order anyone to what he knew would be their deaths. And for the first time in a long time, he felt light, almost buoyant. Now he could live life for a little while.

After a short walk, Nok arrived at his small wedge of a chamber. One of the few remaining pilfered lanterns stood on a ledge outside of the entry, lighting both the corridor and his home. He looked at its warm glow and decided that he would miss some of the benefits of being Commander of the Colony, light not being the least of them. He entered to find the room surprisingly sullen. His fear of tragedy kicked in immediately.

He did a quick scan. Everything seemed in order. Keerka appeared a little tired and Leeg was sitting next to their frequent resident, Kicki. The only thing out of the ordinary was Tearsk. "What's wrong?"

Keerka got up slowly. "Relax, Nok. There's nothing…wrong. But something has come up."

"I don't like when things come up. Things coming up are never good. Just tell me. I don't want to brace for it, I just want to know." After a stern look from Keerka, Nok sat.

"I'm sorry, Commander, I mean, Nok. I didn't know she was a secret. Lydeck was right—I'm a failure at everything." Tearsk got up and ran toward the exit.

"Wait," Nok said, standing to stop him. "You did great today. You saved Leeg. Look at him. My son is alive because of you. You fought well today. Don't let me hear that you're anything but a hero."

"You won't think that when you hear what Kicki saw."

Nok looked at Kicki, who appeared to have aged five years in one day.

She returned his gaze with sadness in her eyes. "Aperion will come. The Royals will come. They will all know soon that I am here. And they will come to claim me or kill me. The colony won't survive unless they are not here when they arrive. The colony will have to abandon the safety of the warrens and go to sea early and stay at sea until a new home is found."

"I didn't know," Tearsk said. "Now we have to leave. Our families have lived here for thousands of generations, and now it'll all be gone, because of me."

"Tearsk, look at me," Nok said, nudging his beak against Tearsk's. "It's just a big rock in the sea. The Royals know about this place, the humans… you know the humans will return one day. The Ancients know we should have abandoned this place a long time ago."

Tearsk looked at the ground. "But it's our home."

"We're Rockhoppers. We'll just hop over to the next big rock in the sea. I believe Commander Trarck will lead us to a great new homeland." Nok looked around the room. "Now, is there anything else? No? All right, Kicki, how much time do we have?"

Kicki stood and swayed only for a moment. "Many tides from now. It's difficult to say with certainty. But we are safe for the time we are here."

"You see? We'll be fine." Nok rested his beak on Tearsk's shoulder. "Thank you. Now go home, hero." He looked back to Kicki. "Is there any chance I will get a little break?"

Kicki closed her eyes and opened them. "Only briefly. A messenger will come for you, and you will go."

Nok shook his head and sighed. "Figured as much."

Keerka stood close to Nok and rubbed his beak with her own. "I knew there was a reason why I chose you as my mate."

"Wait, you chose me? I think you took one too many hits to the head." Nok rubbed beaks with Keerka once more.

"Ugh. Will you two stop that," Leeg said, stepping between them. "I have to ask you something. What will Kicki do? She has to find somewhere safe."

Nok and Keerka sighed simultaneously and Keerka spoke. "I know she will, son. As soon as she's able to, she *will* have to leave and find a safe home."

"I don't want her to leave. She's my friend. She'll be scared and alone." Leeg leaned into his mother's belly.

Nok wedged his flipper between the two. "She won't be alone, son. You will have to go with her and protect her."

Leeg looked at Kicki, who seemed to have drifted into a dreamlike state. "How? I'm not like you. I've never fought anything," he said to Nok.

"You will learn what to do. But don't fret about it now. The time will come when you are ready, and you haven't even begun to molt yet." Nok, Keerka and Leeg stood huddled close together, happy to be safe and together.

Kicki began to stir. She sprang to her feet. With eyes wide, she spoke, "She is my mother's mother."

CHAPTER 51

Trarck, Kairg and Kuk-kek walked through the Council chamber on their search for Ki-ok. "And what makes you think he's there?" Kairg said.

Trarck didn't have a solid answer for him, so he gave his best answer. "It's just a hunch, but I'm pretty sure he is in Packt's old quarters, or at least near there."

"It makes sense," Kuk-kek said. "It's where he first became what he is."

Colonel Kairg puffed his chest. "Well, whether it makes sense or not, I still say it's a fool's errand. He's probably swum half way to the Falklands by now. He made his escape, and he's gone. That's what I would do, at least."

"Then it's a good thing you're not who we're after," Trarck said with his voice trailing away. Someone standing in a Council seat caught his eye. "You go on ahead. I'll catch up."

Kuk-kek watched Trarck hop and climb up the Council seats. "Where's he going?"

Colonel Kairg studied the form in the distance. "Tretak. He's going to see Tretak. Well…good for him," Kairg said. Kuk-kek shrugged and they continued on their way.

"Hey. Hi. How are you feeling?" Trarck said when he reached Tretak.

"I'm feeling good. Thank you again," she said. Trarck shook his head like it was nothing. "You took on a Royal Emperor for me and you killed it; I'm impressed."

"Bah, the big ones fall harder, that's all."

"So have you come here to arrest me?"

"Arrest you? No. If you hadn't done what you did, we might be under Lydeck's rule. So...no chance of me arresting you or anything," he said clumsily.

Tretak snickered a little. "Good, because I'm a lot more formidable than some sorry old Shadow Warrior."

"I don't doubt that." Trarck stared at Tretak for moment. "But I have to ask—why the vendetta against Lydeck? Other than him being...you know...a guano worm."

Tretak looked away for a moment. "We never met before, did we?"

"Not that I recall."

"I lived here before—when the colony was much bigger—so big that there wasn't enough room for us all to nest in the warrens. That's probably why. It was before the war."

Trarck watched her, waiting for her to continue.

Tretak stared at him for a moment then continued talking. "I had a mate then. Krik-kaw was his name. We nested together, and I'd just had two eggs when the humans started coming. At first we were out of harm's way. Our nest was higher up, and they weren't too keen for climbing. But then they came again and this time they did climb. They came at us, doing the awful things men do. I accidentally kicked an egg out of the nest. I wanted to retrieve it, but had no time. We scrambled up the rocks to higher ground. Krik-kaw helped other Rockhoppers up, including Lydeck. As we were climbing up another rock, Lydeck couldn't make it and Krik-kaw helped him. The men were right behind us. As Krik-kaw climbed the rock, Lydeck kicked him back down. A man stuffed him in a sack. I heard him screaming as they beat the sack with a club. Lydeck killed my mate." Tretak looked away.

"After that, I left this place. I had one egg still, but I was forced to abandon it, I couldn't raise a chick alone, and Treeg hadn't taken control yet. I just swam away until hatred got the better of me and I returned. I was surprised by how things had changed. And I was even more surprised to find Lydeck in a position of power. I got in close to him and waited. I learned of all of his plans and instead of killing him outright, which would have got me a date with the Tribunal, I plotted and helped him and set up his fall. I was still going to kill him, but a very big flipper got in the way of that."

Trarck stared at her until the silence became awkward. "You've been through a lot. But things will be different now. You know, a lot of abandoned eggs are taken in by barren couples. Maybe your egg survived to be hatched. You have a seat on the Council—"

"Thank you, Trarck, but no thank you. If my egg did hatch, well, it's their child, not mine. Besides, I have a Rockhopper to hunt down."

"Revenge doesn't change anything. You might find it as empty as popping a kelp bladder."

"Maybe, but it sure is fun popping those things." Tretak hopped down the rocks of the Council and Trarck followed.

"Do you want to at least stay and help me catch Ki-ok?"

"Nah. That poor penguin was used by Lydeck. That doesn't excuse his actions, but he isn't all to blame. You go catch him. I've given Lydeck enough of a head start." She hopped off of the last rock. "Maybe I'll see you around one day, Commander," she said without turning back.

Trarck watched her go. "I would like that."

CHAPTER 52

Trarck joined Kairg and Kuk-kek as they were making the final ascent to Packt's chamber. The wind howled through the break in the wall. Head plumes jostled in the breeze and fatigue gnawed away at their patience.

Colonel Kairg kept looking at Trarck, but Trarck kept ignoring his looks. A few more steps and Kairg looked at him again. Trarck could take no more. "What?" he snapped.

Kairg stopped and gave him an expectant stare. Trarck threw up his wings in frustration. "What do you want? I'm obviously too tired to read your mind."

Kairg grunted. "Well what happened with Tretak? Are you two…well, you know?"

Trarck pulled his head back in surprise. "What? No. We just talked for a little while."

Kairg nodded and resumed walking. "Sorry, I just thought that maybe after today, you might have made a connection."

"No, nothing like that," he said, shaking his head. "She's not staying around. In fact, she's already gone."

"Oh. I'm sorry. Did you at least find out why she did what she did? I mean, she helped Lydeck get elected only to help bring him down. It seems like a lot of trouble if she was going to kill him anyways."

"Yes it was. But from what she told me, it makes some sense. She didn't just want to kill him. She wanted to destroy him. I'll tell you more later. Right now, we need to focus on Ki-ok."

"So she's gone? Do you think she might be going to rejoin Lydeck? They could have been in this together and cobbled together an escape plan if it went awry."

Trarck stopped as if to ponder what Kairg had said. It was plausible, but he doubted that it was true. "No, I'm certain she was telling the truth. Either way, it doesn't matter—she's gone now."

"Quiet," Sergeant Kuk-kek said, while stepping into an alcove. "This is Packt's quarters."

Kairg made a dismissing noise to Kuk-kek. "It would take a big-eared whale to hear anything in this wind."

"Nevertheless," Trarck said as he entered the small chamber. Kairg followed him in while Kuk-kek kept an eye on the path outside.

It only took a moment to find out that Ki-ok wasn't hiding in the darkness. "Any other ideas, Commander sleuth?" Kairg said, pushing his way past Trarck.

Trarck snorted at him. "Get all of your disrespect out now, Colonel. When I become Commander, I'll have you dunked and flogged for insubordination."

"It's not even official yet and he's already drunk with power," Kairg said to Kuk-kek.

Trarck looked at the gap in the cliff wall and let out a prolonged sigh. "He's out there." He pointed to the opening and walked toward it. As he stepped outside, the wind buffeted him. He looked around, carefully examining each moon shadow until he finally spotted the fluttering of Ki-ok's head plume. Trarck nudged Kairg and gestured toward an outcropping overlooking the crashing waves far below.

Kairg and Kuk-kek went left and right and Trarck took the center path. The sea-mist covered the rocky cliff in dew, making climbing difficult. Each step had to be slow and methodical to avoid a slip and a long fall to certain death. After several arduous minutes, the trio stood behind Ki-ok. If he knew they were there, he didn't show it. Trarck looked to his companions, who indicated him to make the arrest. "Lieutenant Ki-ok, by the authority of the Defense Ministry, you are under arrest for the murders of Packt and Eeco. Come with us to face the Tribunal."

Ki-ok didn't budge. He continued to stare at the moon's reflection on the dark blue sea. After several moments, Trarck repeated his statement. Ki-ok looked up to the sky. "It's not my fault. It's not, Colonel."

Kairg looked at Trarck and stepped closer. "It is Ki-ok. You killed Packt and Eeco."

"I know that is. I know." Ki-ok stood and turned to face his captors. "It's not my fault your mate died. She was killed by humans, the Overlord's commands, and our own choice to follow those commands. I didn't refuse to take my company to shore, I followed my orders. I followed them as I was told to do. I could have gone to shore, though I doubt it would have made a difference. Only more Rockhoppers would have died. More would have died. You were correct, Colonel. I was scared. I was very scared. But we're Rockhoppers. We aren't meant to do this. We are not. War? Killing? We are only supposed to swim and eat and have chicks. And then we die and go to the Great Sea. That's all we are meant to do."

"I know her dying wasn't your fault, Ki-ok. You were a reason for the unreasonable. We shouldn't have been there." Kairg looked to Trarck, who stood ready. "I know it's too late, but I don't blame you any longer. But you did commit some very serious crimes. Now, let's go. I will speak on your behalf at the trial; enough have died already."

"No, Colonel. It's too late for that. It's too late. I let Lydeck manipulate me. I let him. But I wanted the glory. I did. I wanted to be seen as more than the coward of the Battle of the Falklands. And I would have done anything to get that. And I did. I did do anything." Ki-ok took a step back from the others.

"Ki-ok," Trarck said. "Nobody else has to die. I will see that the Tribunal doesn't have you executed."

"It doesn't matter now. It doesn't. I did what I did, and I'm as good as dead for it." Ki-ok took another step back. "You were right, Colonel. I am a coward. And I am afraid to face the Tribunal; I am ashamed to face my peers, and I fear tomorrow. I fear."

"We all fear, Ki-ok," said Kairg.

"Ki-ok, wait," Trarck said as Kairg took a step toward him.

Ki-ok looked at Kuk-kek, lowered his head, and took the final step over the edge.

Trarck peered over the cliff and saw Ki-ok and the waves hit the rocks together. He looked to the moon and let out an exhausted breath. He faced Kairg and Kuk-kek. "There's been enough death."

Kairg looked across the moonlit ocean. "Too much, in fact, Commander," he said. "Too much."

CHAPTER 53

Nok and Keerka stood together on top of the rocky seaside mountain known as the Warrens, watching the wind push the fog away to reveal the yellow-white sun.

Keerka sighed and rested against Nok. "Two weeks with nothing happening. It's almost boring around here now."

Nok pulled his head back and looked at her. "I would have thought you would've liked it that way?"

"I do. I have to adjust."

"Well, Trasik-lon and Kerl resigned their Council seats. There's an opening there for you if you get too bored."

She gave Nok a playful slap. "I would have to be really bored to put myself through that hell. No thanks, General."

"Just a suggestion. And don't call me General. It's an honorary title only." Nok grew silent and gazed over the ocean. He watched birds soar on the wind and inhaled the briny air. He enjoyed his retirement. No more pressure or things to do; just live for once. But even as he found peace in the company of Keerka and the embrace of the wind, his heart grew heavy. "Leeg is in his third day of molt. We won't have him for much longer."

Keerka nuzzled her beak against Nok. "I know. But let's enjoy the present and leave tomorrow to its own worries."

"That's why I chose you, you always put me right." Keerka nuzzled her beak a little deeper into his chest. "Ouch. All right, all right. You chose me."

As they sat listening to the wind, Nok's ears picked up an odd sound in the distance. He straightened up, his body growing tense.

"What is it?" Keerka said in alarm.

"Did you hear that? It was a strange thumping sound."

Keerka listened, straining to hear anything against the wind. "I don't hear anything. Maybe a rock broke away and hit the water."

Nok remained silent and wary. "No…that wasn't it. Whatever it was, it's gone now."

"Why don't you just turn off your ears and relax? Or does being a general mean you have to stay on guard?"

Nok gave her a playful warning glare and taking her advice, settled in next to her.

The pair were sitting and dozing in the sun, putting noises and trouble behind for a while, when a call came from behind them. Nok stood and shook his head in frustration. He turned to find Kuk-kek running toward them. "What is it, Sergeant?" Nok said, not masking his annoyance.

"I apologize, General. But Commander Trarck requests your presence immediately."

Nok looked at Keerka. "I never should've accepted this title, honorary or not."

Kuk-kek looked between the two. "I'm sorry, General, but this is urgent."

"And what is so urgent that the Commander needs to interrupt my time alone?"

"A human flying vessel has landed near the north shore. We are mustering the forces as a precautionary measure. He would like your advice."

"The north shore?" Nok said, exchanging worried looks with Keerka.

"Yes sir. Near the former Gentoo Rise."

"Well, you got your excitement," Nok panted to Keerka. "I swear, this never ends."

More from Rockhopper Books

Rise of the Penguins Saga

Rise of the Penguins
Book 1

The Warlord, The
Warrior, The War
Book 2

Crosscurrents
Book 3

The Royal Creed
Book 5

Order of Kings
Book 6

The Great Auk War
Book 7
(coming soon)